"Are y

Sam's heart stirred at the wonder in Juliet's daughter's face. "Sort of..."

"I can ride." Juliet's brother's face lit up. "Raeder's been teaching me."

"Okay, but riding herd on a lively cow pony is a lot different from trotting around the corral on an old rescue horse," Sam pointed out.

"Yeah, but—"

"And with that—" Juliet took her daughter's hand and headed toward the house "—let's not keep Mr. and Mrs. Mattson waiting."

From Juliet's hunched shoulders as she walked, Sam could tell she was still nervous. He was dealing with his own nerves. What did his mom expect to gain from having Juliet and her kids come out to the ranch? Was she trying to be a matchmaker between Sam and a Sizemore?

What had changed her mind about that notorious family from just a few weeks ago, when neither of his parents could say a good word about a single one of them?

Besides, he had no intentions of rekindling his teenage romance with Juliet.

Help her? Yes.

But let himself love her again? *No way.*

Award-winning author **Louise M. Gouge** writes historical and contemporary fiction romances for Harlequin's Love Inspired imprint. She earned a BA in creative writing from the University of Central Florida and a Master of Liberal Studies degree from Rollins College. After teaching English and humanities for sixteen and a half years at Valencia College in Kissimmee, Florida, Louise now writes full-time. Contact Louise at louisemgougeauthor.blogspot.com, Facebook.com/louisemgougeauthor, and on X, @louisemgouge.

Books by Louise M. Gouge

Love Inspired

Safe Haven Ranch
Feuding with the Cowboy

K-9 Companions

A Faithful Guardian

Love Inspired Historical

Finding Her Frontier Family
Finding Her Frontier Home

Four Stones Ranch

Cowboy to the Rescue
Cowboy Seeks a Bride
Cowgirl for Keeps
Cowgirl Under the Mistletoe
Cowboy Homecoming
Cowboy Lawman's Christmas Reunion

Visit the Author Profile page at LoveInspired.com for more titles.

FEUDING WITH THE COWBOY

LOUISE M. GOUGE

LOVE INSPIRED
INSPIRATIONAL ROMANCE

ISBN-13: 978-1-335-62134-4

Feuding with the Cowboy

Recycling programs for this product may not exist in your area.

Love Inspired
22 Adelaide St. West, 41st Floor
Toronto, Ontario M5H 4E3, Canada
www.LoveInspired.com

HarperCollins Publishers
Macken House, 39/40 Mayor Street Upper,
Dublin 1, D01 C9W8, Ireland
www.HarperCollins.com

Printed in Lithuania

If we confess our sins, he is faithful and just to
forgive us our sins, and to cleanse us
from all unrighteousness.
—*1 John* 1:9

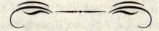

My special thanks go to my wonderful agent, Tamela Hancock Murray, and to my fabulous editor, Shana Asaro. Thank you for all that you do.

As with all of my stories, this book is dedicated to my beloved husband, David, my one and only love, who encouraged me to write the stories of my heart and continued to encourage me throughout my writing career. David, I will always love you and miss you.

Chapter One

"Hi, Sam."

Sam Mattson looked up from the adoption forms on his desk to see a familiar face from his past.

"Juliet Sizemore." Even as he said her name, his pulse kicked into overdrive. He swallowed hard and stared down at his desk again. His first and only love, who'd betrayed him and broken his heart. Even after ten years, he still could feel the pain she'd caused him. It tainted every relationship he'd ever tried to have with a woman.

When he could speak without choking, he muttered, "What brings you here?"

"Well, actually, I was looking for your Cousin Will. Is he around?" Her voice as flippant as in her teens—one of the reasons he'd fallen for her in his own season of rebellion—she glanced out the door of Sam's small office as though Will might walk past in the hallway.

"He's out of town." Sam couldn't keep his gaze from her pretty face. At twenty-eight, she had blossomed into an adult beauty.

"Oh." Her posture slumped, and she let out a sigh. "Well, maybe you can help me." A hint of doubt colored her tone.

Sam grunted. "You want my help?" They locked gazes

for several seconds until she finally broke it off. "The last I heard about you, other than when you stood me up at the crossroads, was when you lied to my Cousin Rob about the woman who rescued his border collie."

"Yeah. Well." Years ago, she would have laughed. Today, she had the grace to blush, the first time he'd ever seen any form of shame on her face. "I was caught off guard when Mr. Mattson bragged about who he was. 'Robert Mattson of the Double Bar M Ranch.'" She did a fairly good job of faking Rob's deep voice. "As you may recall, our families have never gotten along. I guess I just wanted to—"

"Wanted to cause pain where you could." He sat back in his desk chair and crossed his arms. "Sounds as reasonable as any excuse…for a Sizemore."

To his surprise, her eyes took on a sheen. Was she faking those tears? Probably, because she'd obviously come here needing something.

"Look, I wouldn't be here, but I don't know where else to go. I need your legal help. Or preferably Will's."

"Will won't be back for a week." Against his better judgment, he added, "What can I do for you?" He waved a hand to the chair across from his desk, feeling a little guilty he'd not invited her to sit before now. His parents had raised him to be a gentleman, and being courteous was always important, even to the woman who'd broken his teenage heart.

She dropped into the chair. "It's my brother, Jeff." Now she blinked away real tears. "After our dad killed his mom at Christmas, he went into foster care, but the foster parents can't handle him. I'm afraid he'll do something really bad and end up in juvie. I want to get custody of him."

She must have caught the doubt in Sam's face, because she hurried to add, "He listens to me."

Nobody in Riverton had been surprised when Dill Sizemore killed his second wife. The cops had been to their home countless times over the years trying to settle their constant domestic disputes. Brenda should have left Dill, but their codependent relationship seemed to have trapped her. Last thing Sam heard, Dill was sitting in jail awaiting trial. He'd probably be given a lengthy prison sentence, where more than one of his relatives now resided.

Despite the conflicts tumbling through his thoughts and emotions, Sam schooled his expression into a professional facade. "So, how will you prove you can support Jeff?" He scoffed softly. "Most important, how will you control him?"

Juliet flipped her long, dark blond hair over her shoulder in a gesture that seemed more impatient than flirtatious. "Like I said, he listens to me. As for supporting him, won't I get paid as his guardian?" She grimaced and blinked those appealing blue eyes. "I mean, I have a job, of course, but—"

"What's your job? Rob said you got fired from that vet clinic in Santa Fe."

"Yeah." She stared down at her hands. "Dr. Vargas didn't like me telling people how to take care of their pets, even though I earned a pre-vet science degree at Adams State University." She gave him a defensive scowl. "Besides, as you know, I grew up on a working ranch. That taught me everything I need to know about taking care of animals."

"Right." Sam scoffed, a little louder this time. Although he'd also grown up on a ranch, he would never give animal health advice to anybody. He'd tell them to take their sick pets to his veterinarian cousin, Sue. "And your current job?"

She bit her lip. "Billings' Burgers."

Ouch! The burger joint on the edge of Riverton didn't have the best reputation and had been shut down a couple of times for food safety violations.

"Okay." Sam pulled out a legal pad and pen to make notes. "Where do you live?"

She bit her lip again. "On Mama's ranch. Such as it is."

Sam didn't have to ask for details. The ranch had gone downhill fast after Juliet's parents divorced. "So, the ranch went to your mom after the divorce?"

She picked at her fingernails.

Sam set his pen down. "Look, if you expect me to help you get custody of Jeff, you're gonna need a good job and a stable home for him. A home not co-owned by his imprisoned father."

She kept studying her hands. "The ranch has been in Mama's family since the 1930s, so it belongs to her. When Dad left her to marry Brenda, my grandpa, her father, was still alive. Dad never owned it and has no claim to it." She snorted softly. "He only acted like he was a big-time rancher to impress people."

Not sure she was telling the truth, Sam made a note to check the legalities of who actually owned the Murphy ranch. "How does your mom feel about letting Jeff live out there? I mean, if I recall correctly, when Brenda got pregnant with him, that was the reason your parents divorced."

"As you seem to enjoy reminding me." True vulnerability shone in her eyes.

Sam looked away. "I'm sorry. I know that was really hard on you." He'd befriended her back in middle school when nobody else would. By high school, they were secret sweethearts. Studying Shakespeare in English class, they'd joked about being Romeo and Juliet, having to keep their love a secret due to an over 150-year-old feud between their families. The Capulets and Montagues, or even the legendary American Hatfields and McCoys, had nothing on the Mattson–Sizemore feud.

"Yeah, well." She brushed at her damp cheeks. "Mama's come a long way since then. Goes to church and stuff. She's okay with having Jeff live with us." Her voice broke. "Please help us, Sam. I have to take him before Judge Mathis in two days, and Jeff doesn't have anybody else but me."

He stared at her for several seconds. Was he foolish to accept this job? It probably would turn out to be *pro bono*. But with both Will and Rob out of town, he didn't have anybody to ask for advice. If he asked his parents, they'd say no. The Sizemores had done damage to the Mattson family more than once over the last many decades. That's why he and Juliet had kept their teenage romance a secret.

At last he released a long sigh. "Okay. Let's do this. I'll let Judge Mathis know I'm representing you."

"Thanks, Sam. I won't forget it. Here's my cell phone number." She handed him a sticky note, then stood and headed for the door.

"I'll walk you out."

"No, that's okay." She hurried up the hallway toward the reception area, practically running out the front door and down the sidewalk.

Through the storefront window, he watched her climb into a battered green 1984 Chevy Silverado, usually a classic pickup, but this one had seen better days. A sandy-blond-haired child sat in the passenger seat, and Juliet embraced her before starting the truck.

An odd shiver crept up his neck. Who was that kid?

* * *

"Mom, that man's watching you." Sassy stared out the windshield toward Sam's law office.

"It's okay." Juliet shrugged. "He's probably worried Grandma's truck won't start, and it'll make his business look bad with this dilapidated rattletrap parked in front."

Sassy giggled. She was used to Juliet's jokes about their lack of resources. Okay, their poverty. Jokes made it easier for both of them to cope. To her relief, at the turn of the key, the engine turned over without complaint, and she shot Sassy a grin.

"So, Mom." She blinked her bright blue eyes in her cute, sassy way. "Ice cream?"

Juliet cringed inside as she winked at her. "Sure." Determined to keep this little girl's disappointments to a minimum, she would make do without the new mascara she'd saved up for. Nobody cared if her eyelashes were their natural washed-out blond instead of a more attractive light brown.

Sassy turned on the radio and sang along with the country music, her sweet voice soothing Juliet's guilty conscience. It had been hard enough to go to the law office planning to ask Will Mattson for help. Nobody had been in the reception area, so she'd found her way back to the only person on the premises. With the way her life had always gone, of course it had to be Sam.

Her first look at him in ten years had left her breathless. Even more handsome than ever, his light brown hair, tanned cowboy complexion and blue-green eyes pierced right through her attempt at bravado and into her heart. As always, she'd reacted with a flippant, defensive response. In truth, it wasn't his Cousin Rob's bragging about his well-known name and ownership of one of the state's largest cattle ranches that prompted her to lie last year. Lying had been her go-to defense mechanism all her life. That was, until last December when she came home to Mama, who'd found "religion" and convinced Juliet that Jesus Christ was the only answer to all her problems and, most of all, her sin. And there were plenty of sins to confess, not just lying. But would anybody in Riverton and surrounding environs believe she'd changed? That she wasn't like the other Sizemores? Unlikely. She'd been trying to do that all her life. The only person who'd ever believed in her was Sam, but she'd ruined forever any chance for a life of happiness with him.

No use going over the past. Mama said the Apostle Paul had done terrible things, but once he met Jesus and his sins were forgiven, he wrote in the Bible that he could forget the things in his past and move on to become more like Jesus. If the man who wrote most of the New Testament could say that, maybe Juliet could follow his example. Until somebody threw her past in her face. But she'd cope with that when the time came.

After purchasing Sassy's ice cream cone at the drive-through, Juliet steered the truck west from town toward Mama's ranch. In the distance, she saw ranch hand Raeder Westfall leaning on his cane as he worked with the new cowpony in the front pasture. Well, not exactly new. Darby had a good sixteen years on him and had actually been put out to pasture when Mama bought him to keep him out of the glue factory. Adding to her many other softhearted but poor business decisions, Mama had also hired Raeder, a broken-down young cowboy with a real-life sob story.

A Wyoming boy a few years younger than Juliet, he'd done well on the rodeo circuit until his wife died, leaving him with a young son to raise by himself. That was when he got too cautious and had a bad fall from a 2000-pound bucking Brahman bull. The bull trampled his leg, which needed several surgeries to repair. Once he was back on his feet—sort of—Mama let him and little Peanut live in the old bunkhouse. That was Mama. Bringing in strays. Believing their sob stories. Trying to help everybody even when she didn't have much for herself.

After pulling up to the rail fence by the back door, Juliet climbed out of the truck, sighing as she and Sassy headed inside. Without Mama's soft heart, where would they be?

"Hey, you two." Mama stood at the stove stirring her delicious-smelling homemade chili. Sassy danced over to her for a hug. "Love you, sweetie." She kissed Sassy's forehead, then turned to Juliet. "So, what did Will say?"

Juliet grimaced. "He's out of town."

"So, you talked to Sam." A glint in Mama's eye said way too much. More than once, she'd urged Juliet to tell Sam about Sassy, saying the child needed a father in her life. Did Mama honestly think they could get back together after all these years? But Juliet had forbidden her from revealing their secret to anyone, especially Sam. Especially Sassy.

"Yeah. He's gonna look into helping me get custody of Jeff."

Mama tasted the chili, nodded with approval and put a lid on the cast-iron pot. "Good."

"What's good, Gramma? The chili or getting help with Jeffie?" Sassy shot a smarty-pants grin at Mama.

Mama laughed. "Both, Little Miss Big Ears. Now you go wash up, then come help me make the cornbread."

Sassy scampered from the room. Even with her out of earshot, Juliet spoke softly. "Sam says we'll need to prove we have a good home for Jeff. I'm not sure what that means."

"You don't need to worry. When I hired Raeder, he needed to prove the same thing for Peanut. Child Legal Services came out and passed us." She chuckled. "'Course it helped that the social worker is in my Sunday school class."

Juliet went to the silverware drawer and took out the utensils needed for their meal. "And that you retook your maiden name after you divorced Dad. Nobody in these parts wants to do any favors for a Sizemore."

Mama came over and set a hand on Juliet's shoulder. "You don't know that. Sam agreed to help you."

"Reluctantly." Juliet's eyes stung at the memory of Sam's wounded expression when he first laid eyes on her. After all these years, did he still resent her for not following through with their elopement? If only he knew...

"But he's still gonna do it. That's a good first step."

"First step toward what, Mama?" Juliet frowned at her. "You gotta stop these insinuations. Sassy's gonna pick up on them."

Mama just grinned.

"I'm serious."

"Serious about what, Mom?"

Juliet groaned. Of course her bright little daughter returned in time to hear Juliet scold her own mother. This old farmhouse had thin walls. Had Sassy heard anything else?

She would have to be very careful what she said when her daughter was home. And what about Jeff? Would he ferret out the truth about Sassy's father? How could Juliet keep the truth from them without breaking her promise to the Lord to stop lying?

* * *

While driving back to the Double Bar M Ranch, Sam was still berating himself for taking Juliet's case. Not only was his emotional well-being now in serious jeopardy, but he also knew her brother Jeff was a troublemaker. Having to deal with a bratty teenage boy wasn't going to be fun. He'd been one himself, and he wouldn't put anybody through what he'd inflicted on his own parents.

Maybe moving back to the ranch where he'd grown up hadn't been such a good idea after all. For three years after law school, he'd had his own apartment in town. But his nearly sedentary life as a lawyer hadn't done any favors to his physical health. He wanted—*needed*—to get back into the natural exercise of ranch work in the evenings and on weekends. On the other hand, being home meant he'd be a target for Mom and Dad's scrutiny. He could just see them bristling when he mentioned taking on Juliet's custody petition. They were pretty forgiving to most people unless their name was Sizemore. Ten years ago, they'd blown up when they discovered his failed attempt to elope with Juliet, saying her deception was just part of her innate character and he'd been blessed to be shed of her. They'd only forgiven him when he agreed to graduate high school and attend college, then law school. Those days were rarely mentioned, especially since he'd done pretty well for himself in the law office. Would that change once he told them about this new case?

For Mom's part, she'd probably panic over him having anything to do with Juliet. With the recent marriages of cousins Will and Rob—Mom having honed her matchmaking skills through both situations—Sam had become her next target. Not only because he was her only son, but also because she wanted grandchildren and his only sister was busy with her own law career in Albuquerque. But Mom would do anything in her power to keep him from taking up again with his once serious—*only* serious—girlfriend.

One advantage to living back home was Mom's great cooking, which he was reminded of the moment he climbed out of his truck and smelled the aroma of her fantastic roast beef. Even as his belly rumbled with anticipation, he braced himself for the coming confrontation. Sure, he could keep quiet about Juliet, but his parents would sense something was up. Best to face the issue head-on. At the supper table, after Dad said grace, Sam took a deep breath and plunged ahead.

"So, I got a new client today." He cut into a thick slice of roast beef. "You remember Jeff Sizemore? The fifteen-year-old kid whose dad killed his mother at Christmastime?"

Dad paused, forkful of meat halfway to his mouth. "Wait. You took that Sizemore kid on as a client? What were you thinking?"

Mom's eyes narrowed. "So, did this boy come to your office himself, or…"

Count on her to cut to the chase. "No. His sister is petitioning for custody, so—"

"Oh, please." Mom glared at him. "*She*'s your new client, isn't she? Juliet Sizemore! What were you thinking?" She repeated Dad's question.

Sam tried to come up with a way to spin this to make it sound better, but even at almost twenty-nine years old, he knew better than to try to fool his parents. "She wants custody of her brother to keep him out of juvie. He hasn't done well in foster care."

"Surprise, surprise." Mom took a sip of her sweet tea.

The juicy, perfectly seasoned bite of meat in Sam's

mouth did nothing to improve the matter. Did Jeff, or Juliet for that matter, ever get to eat prime beef like this? He recalled her look of desperation as she asked for his help, and his well-heeled life suddenly soured his appetite.

"Every kid needs every possible chance to get past the troubles in their lives." Sam eyed each parent in turn. "You taught me that, remember? We may not think much of the Sizemores, but maybe we can do something for Jeff that will make a difference. I mean, his mother was killed right in front of him. When Dill comes to trial, Jeff will have to testify against him. We Mattsons have had our troubles, but nothing like that."

His parents ate silently for a few minutes, so Sam forced down a few bites, too. Finally, Mom spoke up.

"All right. I'm proud of you for wanting to help the less fortunate. I'm glad you chose family law instead of moving to the city with your sister and working in more lucrative corporate law. I know you and Will have helped a lot of people."

Sam could hear it coming. "But?"

Dad answered. "Just don't let that girl, that woman, get her hooks back into you. She'll just hurt you again."

Sam took another bite of meat to avoid responding with a quick dismissal of his parents' concerns. Not when he had the same fear. Looking into Juliet's bright blue eyes this afternoon had done something to his emotions. How would he manage to keep her from reaching his heart?

Chapter Two

"Wait here." Juliet waved Jeff to a chair outside the judge's chambers. "This shouldn't take long. Right, Sam?" She tried to smile, but it felt more like a grimace. Would her brother mind her?

To her relief, Jeff did as she said but with a scowl. "You promised me we'd get burgers after this, right? And not those cardboard fakes at Billings' Burgers. I want one from Mattsons' Steakhouse." He shot a defiant look at Sam, who stood several yards away, looking as uncomfortable as Juliet felt.

He shrugged. "Sure. Why not."

Juliet swallowed hard. Did Sam realize that meant he would be buying? Like their dad, Jeff knew how to manipulate people, taking casual remarks as promises, then bullying a person until they did what he wanted. Despite her claims to Sam, she couldn't expect Jeff to behave any better for her. But she'd have to face that problem when the time came. Right now she had a more serious issue to deal with. Fifteen years ago, Judge Mathis had been the one to decide thirteen-year-old Juliet would remain with her mother rather than move to town with her dad. Dill and Brenda hadn't been happy about it. They'd counted on Juliet to look after their new baby, Jeffie, so they could continue their "busy" lives, which usually included a lot of partying. How would the judge view Juliet's less than stellar life after that decision?

"The judge will see you now." The dark-haired young female assistant held the door open for Juliet and Sam.

In her well-worn jeans and faded green blouse, Juliet had felt out of place the moment they'd walked into the courthouse. This woman's pristine black business suit, white blouse and flawless professional hairdo—not to mention Sam's black dress jacket, white shirt and black bolo tie—intensified Juliet's discomfort. Was this black-and-white combo some sort of uniform these legal types wore? Actually, Sam also wore dressy jeans and polished Western boots, but then, everybody wore jeans and boots around here.

On shaky legs, she entered the judge's chambers, with Sam close on her heels. The room smelled of old books and furniture polish.

"Good afternoon, Mr. Mattson, Miss Sizemore. Have a seat." The graying judge indicated the two brown leather chairs in front of her large, well-oiled oak desk. Once they were seated, she peered down at the papers on her desk, then looked at Juliet over the rims of her reading glasses. "So, Miss Sizemore, tell me why I should grant you custody of your brother." Her tone was businesslike and impersonal, but her eyes bored into Juliet's.

"As you can see from the letter, Judge—" Sam said.

"Mr. Mattson, I didn't ask you. Let your client answer."

Juliet gulped. How many of her relatives, both ancestors and still living, had faced Riverton judges since the first one was hanged as a cattle rustler in 1887? Since childhood, she'd tried to rise above the Sizemores' disreputable and illegal actions by sticking to the law. But like an anchor, her family's unsavory reputation always seemed to pull her back under the waves of borderline criminal behavior.

Lord, please help me. She was new to praying, but maybe God would help her now.

"Ma'am—" Her voice squeaked oddly, and Sam patted her arm. A reassuring warmth radiated from his touch and traveled upward into her heart. She inhaled a bracing breath. "I know Jeff's caused some problems for folks, but I love him, and he listens to me." Not that he obeyed, but he did listen. "My mother is willing to have him live with us at the ranch. I believe we can turn his life around."

"Humph." The judge perused the papers again. "It says here you want to give full disclosure concerning any possible impediments to my granting you custody."

Juliet glanced at Sam. He didn't smile but did give her a little nod. She gulped again.

"Judge Mathis, I haven't always been truthful, and it's caused some trouble for some folks. But I've come to Jesus with all my heart and, reading where the Bible says to put off falsehood and tell the truth, the first bad thing He took out of my life was lying."

The judge blinked. "Hmm." She looked at her papers again and seemed to be hiding a smile. Was that good or bad? "Tell Jeff to come in here."

Sam went to the door and called to Jeff. Jeff shuffled in wearing his usual defiant expression.

"Sit down," the judge said.

He obeyed, maybe because part of being a Sizemore meant you knew you had to do what the judges said or get the worst end of the stick. Or it could have been Sam's imposing six-foot-two height towering over him that made him obey the judge.

"Now, Jeff, your sister wants custody of you. Do you know what that means?"

"Yeah." He snorted out a laugh.

The judge glared at him.

"Say 'yes, ma'am.'" Juliet glanced nervously at the judge.

"Yes, ma'am."

"That's better. Now, what do you think, Jeff? I know you weren't happy with the Simpsons—"

"Yeah, but they were—"

"You don't have to explain." The judge's voice had a hard edge. "Do you want to live with Juliet and Mrs. Murphy?"

He shrugged. "I suppose."

She sighed. "All right. I'm giving you a trial period." She turned to Juliet. "Jeff can live with you and your mother at the ranch until the end of the school year, with the stipulation that Mr. Mattson will be closely involved in his activities. If the three of you can keep him out of trouble that long *and* I see the difference in him myself, I'll make it permanent." She removed and folded her glasses and used them as a pointer as she spoke to Jeff. "Your part in this is to obey your guardians and stay out of trouble. Do you understand?"

Rubbing his palms on the wooden chair arms, Jeff didn't meet her stern gaze. "Yessum."

The judge faced Juliet again. "Are you sure you want to do this?"

Her heart skipping with happiness, Juliet smiled. "Yes, ma'am. I surely do."

"Very well." She signed a paper on her desk. "It's done. Have a good day."

For several seconds, Juliet couldn't move. Sam nudged her arm. "Let's go."

"Mr. Mattson," the judge said. "A word."

Sam gave Juliet a nod. "I'll be right out." He turned to Jeff. "Then we'll go get that hamburger."

Despite her discomfort over Sam's falling for Jeff's earlier manipulative demand, she couldn't stop the tickle near her heart. He didn't have to buy hamburgers for them, but maybe it was his attempt to win Jeffie over. She could live with that.

With Judge Mathis's admonition—to keep careful track of Jeff and personally involve him in healthy activities—foremost in his thoughts, Sam followed Juliet's beat-up old junker to his family's steakhouse and pulled his new Ford F-150 into the space beside her. It was late afternoon, and only a couple of cars were parked there. Good. The fewer people who saw him with Juliet, the better. Being with Jeff posed no problem for him. Folks were used to seeing Sam with kids who were in the middle of family disruptions. Unfortunately for him, Juliet and Jeff would now have to be inseparable outside of the boy's hours in school. That might prove dangerous for Sam's sense of well-being. Or, more like, dangerous to his heart.

He texted his mother to let her know not to save supper for him, then got out of his pickup as Jeff jumped out of Juliet's truck, a smug look on his face. Sam knew exactly what the boy had done in saying he wanted to eat here. He wanted to show the town he'd somehow bested the Mattsons. Fat chance. Sam would show him…

No, that wasn't right. He'd struggled with this whole situation from that moment two days ago when he'd agreed to help Juliet. But he couldn't take it out on Jeff. His job was to try to reform the kid, not to best him or condemn him. What would have helped Sam in his rebellious years? Not criticism, that was sure. Every time Mom or Dad yelled at him or pointed to Sadie, his perfect little sister, as an example, it only made Sam angrier and more obstinate. And being a Mattson meant the community either tolerated or ignored his recklessness.

Sometimes the deputies didn't even stop him when he sped through town or out on the highway. When they did stop him, they just gave him a warning or waved him off once they saw who he was. Only by the Lord's grace had Sam never caused serious damage to anything or anyone. Then, after Juliet broke his heart, he'd finally grown up and improved his behavior, so these days, everybody respected Sam, and nobody ever mentioned those years of rebellion and mistakes.

In contrast, Jeff had suffered condemnation his entire fifteen years simply because he was a Sizemore. In the less than two months since Dill killed Brenda, things only got worse. Not that the community blamed Jeff for his father's actions, but they also didn't support him as they would have many other kids in the same circumstances, mainly because he was already a troublemaker following in his family's ways. Last fall at the high school's homecoming dance, Cousin Rob had caught Jeff and his pals planning to trip Zoey Parker, a sweet little gal with cerebral palsy, who was the daughter of Sam and Will's paralegal—and now Rob's stepdaughter. That kind of meanness was imbedded deep in a person's soul. How could Sam help a kid like that? All he could do was pray for wisdom.

Inside the aroma-filled restaurant, as he removed his Stetson, the staff greeted him with their usual friendly remarks…until they saw Juliet and Jeff. Eyes widened with surprise and questions.

"Welcome to Mattsons' Steakhouse, folks." Ruth, the hostess on duty, seemed to force a smile as she grabbed three menus and three sets of utensils rolled in black cloth napkins. "Follow me." The forty-something woman led them to a booth at the back of the dining room and laid two menus on the side of the table with its back to the room, and one on the side facing out, then winked at Sam. Clever lady. She knew just how to place people at these tables.

"Thanks, Ruth." Sam took the seat facing the room and set his hat beside him. Not only would that keep either of his guests from sitting beside him, but he'd also be able to watch their sibling relationship. Did Jeff really listen to Juliet, as she claimed? Or did he use the usual Sizemore tactics to try to manipulate his sister?

"Mmm." Juliet inhaled a deep breath. "Smells so good in here, doesn't it, Jeff?"

Jeff didn't answer, just stared around the dining room, as he scooted into the booth, his eyes wide as he took in the Western decor. Once he was seated, his belligerent expression returned. "I want a steak. With fries and a Coke. And an appetizer."

"Now, Jeff—" Juliet began.

"It's okay." Sam wouldn't let the scolding start…yet. "I'm hungry, too. We'll have an early supper."

Ruth nodded. "I'll get your server." She waved to Stacy, a high school senior who worked here after school.

The girl hurried over. "Hey, Mr. Mattson." She noticed the others, and a frown crossed her face. She quickly brightened her expression. "What can I get y'all to drink?"

"Hey, Stacy." Jeff smirked as he looked up at the girl. "Surprised to see me here?"

"Hey, Jeff." To her credit, she didn't take the bait, but kept a lilt in her voice. "Drinks?"

"I want a Coke," Jeff said. "A big one."

"Sweet tea, please." Juliet smiled at Stacy.

"Coffee for me," Sam said. "Thanks, Stacy."

"I want the cheese fries appetizer." Jeff tapped the menu. "And the coconut shrimp."

Stacy looked at Sam, and he nodded his consent. "I'll get those right out."

While they waited, they continued to study the menu. Once Stacy brought the drinks and appetizers, Jeff grabbed a fry and shoved it in his mouth.

"Ready to order?" Stacy asked.

"Give us another minute."

"Sure." Stacy moved to another table.

"Let's pray." Sam bowed his head, not waiting for the others. With thanks offered for the food, he lifted his head to see Juliet had bowed hers, but Jeff had kept eating.

Seeing hesitation in Juliet's eyes as she scanned the menu, Sam said, "Order whatever you like."

A slight frown crossed her brow, but she answered, "Thanks."

Stacy returned, notepad in hand. "Ready?"

As Sam expected, Jeff ordered the most expensive steak and every extra he could read off the menu. Stacy wrote the items on her notepad but kept glancing at Sam. He nodded each time. Never mind that this would blow his carefully crafted budget for eating out this month, a budget necessary because of his pricey truck payments. But when the main course arrived, he didn't regret coming here.

Jeff had gobbled down most of the appetizers as though he hadn't eaten in a week. Yet when he stared at his steak like he couldn't quite believe it was for him, then dug in without his usual sullen defensiveness, Sam felt a slight shift in his thoughts about the kid. Even Juliet seemed to relish each bite as though unused to a good steak. As before, he recalled that these two hadn't lived with an abundance of food or material possessions, as he had.

After eating half her meal, Juliet set a hand on Jeff's arm. "You don't have to finish it all."

"No, I gotta eat it. I'm not gonna let them throw it away."

"Silly boy." Juliet laughed. "You can take it home and eat it later. That's what I'm gonna do."

Jeff stared at her for a moment. "No way."

"Yes, way."

Sam's view of Jeff shifted a little more. Who hadn't heard of restaurant doggie bags? Jeff, obviously. His reactions to every part of this experience suggested he'd never even been to a fancy restaurant before. Hadn't Dill ever taken his family out to eat? What else had he neglected in his son's upbringing? And from Juliet's clear enjoyment, it must be a rare treat for her. When they were in high school, he'd wanted to bring her here for a special date, but that would have exposed their secret relationship. Instead, he'd saved his allowance and drove her to the fancy La Fonda restaurant in Santa Fe. What should be a happy memory for him only stirred up grief over how foolish he'd been to believe she loved him. Besides, that was long, long ago, and a lot of brackish water had flowed under the metaphorical bridge of their lives since then.

Sam couldn't change their pasts, but maybe with the Lord's help, he could change the course of their futures. Part of that would be replacing Jeff's bad behaviors with good ones, and Sam had a good idea where to start. As he drove behind Juliet out to the Murphy ranch, the idea grew, along with his enthusiasm. Now, if her mother, Petra—and

Juliet, of course—agreed, this might just be the perfect project to put Jeff on the road to redemption.

After Sam's insistence that she order whatever she wanted, Juliet had ordered a larger steak so she could take some home to Mama. Even though Mama raised a few dozen steers each year, she couldn't afford to butcher any of them for her own consumption. The sale of those steers had to last her the entire year, along with the meager proceeds from the hay she grew on the south fifteen acres. Now with Jeffie, Sassy and Juliet to feed, Mama would have to further stretch her budget. Juliet would be willing to get a second job if she didn't have to be free to manage Jeffie's actions after school. Where could she get a job with that kind of flexibility?

Back at Mama's ranch, she waited for Sam to pull in beside her before heading into the house. Jeffie carried in his school backpack and a ragged duffel bag containing his clothes. He'd missed school today for the meeting with the judge, but she'd make sure he caught up with his classes and help him if he needed it with his homework. Except statistics. She'd never mastered that subject.

"Come on in," she called to Sam as he climbed out of his fancy, shiny new blue Ford F-150 Lariat. The truck suited him. He jogged up the back walk looking more like the cowboy he was, having shed the formality of his black jacket, tie and white shirt. His light blue t-shirt and darker windbreaker were reflected in his blue-green eyes, those penetrating eyes being one of the reasons she'd fallen for him back in middle school. Plus his listening ears. He'd paid attention to her when nobody else would. Only after a few years of contemplation did she admit to herself that he might have been more interested in defying his family by consorting with a Sizemore than in actually caring about Juliet herself. Or maybe that was her way of forgiving herself for not fighting harder to keep her promise to elope with him. Or maybe she just wasn't being fair. No doubt over the past ten years, he'd grown up, as she had. And together they had to make sure Jeffie didn't make the same mistakes they, or her infamous family, always seemed determined to make.

Entering the kitchen, where Mama's chicken soup simmered in the big pot on the ancient propane stove, she glanced around for her daughter.

"She's helping Raeder with Peanut," Mama whispered.

Relief flooded Juliet's chest. Mama read her well. Now if Sassy would just stay out of the house until Sam left, all would be well.

"You boys come on in. Sam, it's good to see you." Mama brushed a hand through her prematurely graying hair, leaving a track of white flour, and waved both of them into the kitchen. "Just finishing up some cookies for Jeffie. You like peanut butter cookies, Jeffie?"

"Don't call me Jeffie." By the time he'd finished the sentence, he had softened his tone, maybe because the aroma of the cookies and chicken soup permeated the air. Or maybe because of Sam squeezing his shoulder. "Yeah, I like peanut butter cookies."

"That's 'yes, ma'am,' Jeff." Sam gave him a stern look. "First thing on your list of changes is speaking to adults respectfully."

"Oh, he's okay—"

"No, please, Mama." Juliet remembered all too well how her mother had never corrected her. "Judge's orders."

Mama blinked. Then winked at Jeffie. "Oh. Okay. So, Jeffie, um, Jeff, do you like peanut butter cookies?"

Jeffie rolled his eyes. "Yes, *ma'am*." She held out a plate-ful, and he grabbed several, eating one right away despite his huge supper at the restaurant.

"Save room for supper," Mama said.

"Sorry, Mama. We already ate. And I brought you something." Juliet handed her the paper sack labeled "Mattsons' Steakhouse."

"Oh, my!" Mama's eyes got red. "You didn't have to do that." She took the two Styrofoam boxes out of the bag and set them on the Formica counter, then opened one.

"Hey, that one's mine." Jeffie grabbed the container.

Juliet gasped. "Jeff, that's so rude. Mama's not gonna steal your food. Look." She took a marking pen from a holder on the counter and wrote his name on the box, then stuck it in the fridge. "There. It's safe."

"It better be." He scowled. "So where am I gonna sleep?" He downed another cookie.

"Got a room all fixed up for you." Forcing a cheerful tone, Mama pointed toward the hallway. "Stairs are that way. Your room is on the right. Sam, you want to go up with him?"

"Sure. Thanks, Miss Petra." He took the width of the kitchen in two long-legged steps. "Hold up, Jeff. Miss Petra, how do you want Jeff to address you?"

Mama blinked. "Why, I hadn't thought about it." A sweet vulnerability crossed her expression. "I wouldn't mind 'Mama,' but—"

"How about 'Miss Petra,'" Juliet said quickly before Jeff could give voice to the sneer on his face. "That's the cowboy way, right, Sam?"

"Yes, ma'am." He grinned, and her heart hiccupped. *Uh-oh.* "And the cowboy code says a cowboy always treats ladies with respect. Got that, Jeff?"

Jeff grunted. "Whatever." He walked into the hallway muttering, "I ain't no cowboy." In seconds, his footsteps sounded on the treads.

Sam patted Mama on the shoulder, and her eyes reddened again. "We're going to make this work, Miss Petra. You just watch." Then he followed Jeffie upstairs.

Mama cleared her throat and stepped over to the stove. "Once I feed Sassy and the Westfall boys, I can cool the leftovers and put them in the fridge for tomorrow."

The disappointment in her voice stung Juliet's heart. Mama was so proud of her delicious chicken soup. By bringing Jeffie here, had Juliet just opened her dear mother up to a boatload of hurt?

Chapter Three

Sam looked around the small, tidy bedroom. A single bed covered with a faded patchwork quilt and throw pillows. A desk complete with lamp and chair and shelves over it holding an old dictionary and a well-read Bible. An overstuffed chair for lounging. A few framed stock pictures of cowboys and cattle hung against the old Western-themed wallpaper. Petra had put a lot of care into this space. But then, she'd always been a decent, kindhearted woman. Why she ever took up with Dill Sizemore all those years ago was anybody's guess.

Watching Jeff take in the furnishings, Sam asked, "What do you think?"

Jeff shrugged. He dropped his backpack and duffel bag near the closet door, then plopped his five-foot-nine body—with a physique made for football or steer wrestling—onto the bed with a *whump!*

Sam pulled out the desk chair, straddled it backward and crossed his arms on the back. "Okay, here's the deal. The judge told me to find some activities that will keep you out of trouble. I have a good plan to keep you occupied so you won't have time for your usual mischief."

Jeff gave him a withering look. "Oh, yeah? What's that, *cowboy*?"

The disdain in his tone set Sam's teeth on edge, but he refused to answer in kind.

"Hey, watch it." He chuckled. "Your family's always been cowboys, just like mine." He knew the second the words were out of his mouth that he'd said the wrong thing.

Jeff sat up and swung his lanky legs over the bedside. "You leave my family out of this. If your family hadn't been out to get us since the 1800s, maybe we'd have a twenty-thousand-acre ranch, too." He scoffed. "We all know what your ancestors did, hanging Jeb Sizemore over a stupid misunderstanding, sayin' he was a cattle rustler when he was just a cowpoke trying to make a livin' for his family."

Sam looked down at his hands. "Well, I'm sure we've all heard that history in a way that makes our own folks look good." He grunted. In truth, who knew what happened some hundred and fifty years ago? "Let's set all that aside and see what we can do to improve your life in the here and now."

"Yeah?" Jeff lay back down again. "So what's your big idea?"

"You're going to join 4-H and raise a steer." Sam could see the kid trying to hide the sudden flicker of interest in his eyes. "The animal will be your responsibility from the time it's weaned from its mama to the day when it competes at the county fair. What do you think?"

Jeff shrugged as he leaned back against the pillow, but his scowl was definitely gone.

"Good. I'll take you out to the Double Bar M Ranch this Saturday, and we'll find the right animal for you." He'd considered asking Miss Petra to provide a calf, but her small herd was Shorthorn, and Mattsons raised Angus, which usually won at the fair.

The scowl returned. "I don't want to go out there. You pick for me."

Sam didn't blame him for wanting to avoid the rest of the Mattson clan. He'd threatened to hurt Zoey last fall, and none of the family wanted him anywhere near her.

"Nope. You need to learn how to pick the most promising animal for your 4-H project. You're going to learn this from stem to stern."

"Stem to stern?" Jeff snorted. "A nautical idiom's pretty stupid for a cowboy to use, Boss."

Sam laughed out loud. "What do you know about idioms? Or anything nautical?"

"I pay attention in English class."

Good to know. "Okay, so, you got a better idiom for learning about raising a steer?"

"Not right away, but I'll be thinking about it."

"You do that." Sam watched him for a few seconds. "Now, on another topic. You will show respect for your sister and Miss Petra, and you do what they say, or you'll answer to me *and* Judge Mathis. They're sacrificing a lot to have you live out here, so you'll help with any chores they tell you to do. I don't know, don't want to know, why you didn't get along with the Simpsons, but these ladies are your family—"

"*Miss* Petra ain't my family."

Sam huffed out a breath. The kid claimed to pay attention in English class but still used improper grammar. "Okay, but that's all the more reason to respect her. She fixed up this room for you." He waved a hand to take it in. "She didn't have to do that, so you'll show her your appreciation. You got that?"

Jeff sat up again and stared hard at Sam. "I got that.

And you better get this. You stay away from my sister. You better not break her heart again. You got that?"

Sam stared at him for a full ten seconds. It would be pointless to tell this kid it was his sister who'd hurt *him*. Once again, it was a version of a family story that favored its own.

"Well, I can't exactly stay away from her because we're both responsible for you and need to work together. But don't worry. We'll keep it professional." He pointed to Jeff's backpack. "Now, get your homework done." He wanted to tell him to work on his grammar, but too many Mattsons said "ain't," as did most of their ranch hands, for that rule to hold up. "See you tomorrow."

"Whatever."

As Sam walked down the stairs, he heard childish giggling. In the kitchen, the same girl he'd seen in Juliet's truck a few days ago sat at the table eating chicken soup with Raeder Westfall and his four-year-old son.

"Miss Petra, this is the best soup I've eaten in a long spell." Raeder spoke with a slight drawl. "Ain't it good, Peanut?" He ruffled his son's hair, and the four-year-old gave him a silly grin. "Now you finish your soup so's you can have one of those peanut butter cookies."

Juliet stood behind the girl, who looked like her mini-me. Who was this kid? And why did Juliet have that deer-in-the-headlights look on her face?

"Hey, Sam." She spoke as if they hadn't spent the entire afternoon together. "You haven't met my daughter, Sassy. Sassy, say hey to Mr. Mattson."

"Hey, Mr. Mattson," the kid said around her bite of chicken.

"Hey, Sassy. Where'd you get that cute name?"

The girl looked up over her shoulder at her mom. "Dunno."

"It's a nickname."

"Ah. Cute." Why was he repeating himself? "How old are you, Sassy?" Wasn't that what adults were supposed to ask kids?

"She's—" Juliet started to speak, then bit her lip.

As Sam waited for her answer to his foolish question, a sick feeling swirled in his belly. He didn't really want to know Sassy's age. When they were dating, they'd always been real careful so they wouldn't make a baby. If Sassy was close to ten years old, that meant Juliet had been dating some other guy, somebody not so careful, at the same time she claimed Sam was her one and only love. No wonder she hadn't shown up for their elopement. She'd lied to him all along, just like all the Sizemores.

Juliet used to lie without a thought. But, as she'd told Judge Mathis, God had shown her a better way, so she wasn't about to revert to her old habits. "She's a little over nine." That still sounded like a lie. "Nine and a half."

From the hurt she saw in Sam's eyes, she had a feeling he was counting backward and coming up with the wrong conclusion.

"Hey, Sam." To Juliet's relief, Raeder stood up and reached out to Sam, saving her from having to say anything more. "How's it going?"

"Pretty good." Sam tore his gaze away from Sassy and shook Raeder's hand. "I guess you know what's going on here with Jeff Sizemore, right?"

"Yep. Anything I can do to help?"

"Just keep an eye on him to make sure he doesn't cause any damage around here."

"Oh, now, Sam." Mama shook a finger at him, but added her characteristic smile. "You give that boy a chance. He may surprise you."

"I can only hope."

"And you can pray." Mama shook her finger at him again, like an old-timey schoolmarm.

"Yes, ma'am."

"Thanks for watching Sassy for me, Raeder." Juliet wished Sam would leave. Maybe if she started a conversation with Raeder about Mama's ranch work, he'd take the hint.

"No problem, Miss Juliet. She was a big help keeping Peanut busy while I worked on the tractor. Gotta get it ready for spring plowing." He gave a shake of his head. "Man, that beast is a pain." He looked at Sam. "You know what I mean?"

Sam grunted. "Sure do. Seems like just when you need a piece of machinery the most, it breaks down. Good thing you're a good mechanic."

"I try."

While the men discussed the woes of unreliable machinery, Juliet couldn't help but doubt the Mattsons ever had such problems. Couldn't they just go buy a new tractor or combine? Mama had to make do with what she'd had for years, equipment her parents had used for years, even before she married Dill. So, she was blessed to have a ranch hand who could fix anything, from motors to fence rails.

She pulled Sassy into a side hug. "Sweetheart, as soon as you finish that cookie, it's time to do your homework. I'll come up in a bit to help you. Then I'll read you a story and hear your prayers."

"Yes, ma'am." Sassy practically inhaled the cookie, then

brushed crumbs from her hands over the sink. "Bye, Peanut. See you tomorrow."

"See you." The sweet little guy gazed adoringly at Sassy. After his own mother passed away, Mama said he acted like a lost puppy, another reason she'd hired Raeder after his rodeo accident, hoping to help the little boy. Once Juliet and Sassy moved here, he'd latched on to Sassy like she was his big sister. Juliet could live with that. Her daughter needed a younger friend who looked up to her.

What she couldn't live with was Sam staring at her and her daughter like he was trying to figure things out. How foolish she'd been to involve him with her family. But needing his help to get custody of Jeffie, what else could she have done?

"Will y'all excuse me?" Sam stepped toward the door. "I still have to milk the cows, so I'd better hightail it out of here."

"I didn't know you milk the cows at your place." Juliet couldn't stop the question. "Don't you have hired help to do that?"

He gave her a look that came close to withering. "There's a lot you don't know about me."

She could all too easily answer back with the same words, but that would be a huge mistake.

He plopped his black Stetson on his head. "See you later, Miss Petra. Sassy. Raeder." He winked at Raeder's little boy. "See you later, Peanut." Then he made his exit.

"Well, I better get to milking, too." Raeder grabbed his cane and reached out to his son. "Let's go, Peanut."

"Hang on a minute," Juliet said. "I want Jeffie to learn how to milk." She stepped into the small hallway outside the kitchen. "Hey, Jeffie. I need you to come down here. And bring your jacket." Back in the kitchen, she had a moment of doubt. "Raeder, do you mind? If he gives you any trouble, just holler. I'll set him straight."

Raeder snorted out a laugh. "Miss Juliet, I've been around folks like the Sizemores all my life." He cleared his throat. "No offense to you, ma'am, being a Sizemore and all. But your brother ain't no different from any other rascally teenager I've met up with. I can manage him."

"Whaddaya want?" Jeffie slunk into the room.

Juliet started to smack his arm for his attitude, but stopped herself. Their dad had hit both of them all too often in the name of discipline. When Juliet lived in Alamosa, Mama kept her informed, knowing she loved her little brother. Most of all, Juliet wanted Jeff to feel safe here.

"Raeder's gonna milk the cow, so you go with him and start learning how to do it."

"Milk a cow?" He tried to scowl at Raeder, but Juliet could see a tiny hint of interest in his eyes. He scoffed. "Can't be too hard if he can do it. Let's go."

"What do you mean, if I can do it?" Raeder laughed again as he ruffled Jeffie's hair like he did his own little son. "Dude, you got a lot to learn."

To Juliet's shock, Jeffie laughed, too, as he brushed Raeder's hand away. "We'll see."

With Peanut hanging on to his dad's hand, they walked out, Raeder carefully leaning on his cane with each step.

"I'm glad Raeder didn't rise to Jeffie's insult," Mama said.

"Me, too." More than that, she was happy and surprised Jeffie not only didn't get mad but also laughed with the ranch hand. Maybe that was a clue for how to handle him, trading harmless insults like most cowboys she knew seemed to do. Before leaving town, she'd noticed Dad and Brenda rarely laughed or even appeared to enjoy life. Growing up in that serious atmosphere, Jeffie could do with some lightening up.

She'd give it a try, but how would Sam take it? Would he approve, or would he find it frivolous? When they were dating, they used to laugh together all the time. His sense of humor was one of his charms. But mostly she fell for him because he listened to her and truly cared about her pain over her parents' divorce. If he'd forgotten how to laugh, that was probably her fault for breaking his heart. But it was too late to do anything about that long-ago hurt.

Or was it? They might not rekindle their teenage love, but maybe they could become friends. *Lord, please show me how to do that.*

"What do you think you're doing, Sam?" Cousin Rob posted his fists at his waist and stared across Sam's desk in the law office. "Helping a Sizemore. And Juliet, of all people, after all the trouble she's caused everybody and to you especially? What's got into you?"

Lauren, Rob's new wife and Sam's former paralegal, stood beside him, puzzlement written across her pretty face. "Let's hear him out, sweetheart. I'm sure he has a good reason."

Rob snorted. "You say that after she tried to ruin your reputation?"

Lauren shook her head. "She didn't even know me except as a client at the vet clinic. It was you she was trying to hurt."

"Just like every Sizemore tries to do whatever harm they can to anybody named Mattson."

"I know that," Sam said. Thirteen years younger than Rob and having always looked up to him—even more so when Rob married Lauren and adopted her sweet daughter, Zoey—Sam rarely challenged Rob on any issue. How could he explain why he'd taken on Juliet's case when he didn't understand it himself? "But maybe this is a chance to help her turn her life around, not to mention Jeff's."

"A kid like Jeff?" Rob grunted. "I told you how he and his gang wanted to hurt Zoey just for meanness' sake. It'll take something mighty powerful to root out that kind of cruelty. Just like their lying, meanness is born and bred into every Sizemore I've ever met."

"That's just it, Rob," Sam said. "A mighty powerful thing called the love of God changed me, and now it's changed Juliet." He hadn't planned to say that, but kept on going. "You know how her mother used to be. Kind-hearted as she always was, Petra could outdrink any cowboy and outcuss any sailor. Then she started coming to church and gave her life to Jesus. I believe that's what's happened to Juliet."

"Oh, isn't that wonderful?" Lauren looked up at her new husband with an adoring gaze. Their mutual love was written all over both of them. "Honey, you know how the Lord helped us through our rough patch. Let's give Juliet a chance to prove herself."

Rob turned an equally adoring gaze toward his bride. "Sweetheart, for you, I'll do anything." He turned a far-from-adoring scowl toward Sam. "Look, if you just did their legal work, it might not be a problem. But with the judge ordering you to be directly involved, you'd better watch out for any of their devious tricks."

"He will." Lauren, always positive, gave Rob a saucy grin. "Now, can we go eat? I'm starving. Come with us, Sam?"

"No, but thanks. I have a bunch of things to catch up on before Will gets back." He gave her a smirking smile.

"Seems our paralegal's gone and gotten herself a new job, so I have to take up the slack."

"Do you need my help?" Lauren leaned over the desk to study the papers spread out in front of him. "I could work a few hours—"

"Now, sweetheart," Rob broke in. "We agreed you'd stay home for the kids now that Mom's moved to Phoenix. Besides, I need you to take care of that pesky ranch paperwork I can't seem to keep up with."

"Sorry." Lauren gave Sam an apologetic shrug. If he was truthful, he thought she looked relieved.

"No problem, Cuz. Y'all go enjoy your lunch."

She grinned, obviously pleased at his use of "Cuz," a nickname all the Mattsons called their many relatives.

After they left, he tried to get back into the matters before him, but his mind kept shifting out to the Murphy ranch, where he'd be spending the last part of his day. Oddly, as much as he dreaded having to deal with Jeff, he looked forward to seeing Juliet again.

Which only proved what Rob had hinted at. He was his own worst enemy.

Chapter Four

Juliet let Sassy off at Riverton Elementary School, where she'd enrolled her at the first of the year. It still pinged her heart to see her spunky little daughter march up to the building, head held high and greeting every kid she passed. She prayed Sassy would make a friend or two, even though she still missed her friends in Santa Fe. At least at her former school, she didn't have to face the prejudice against her last name. They'd talked about it and prayed though. And Sassy, true to her name, faced it with courage, determined to prove herself to one and all as a good person and a good student. Only time would tell whether she could conquer the prejudice, or if it would conquer her. *Lord, please help her...*

"So, you gonna drive me to school or sit here wastin' gas?" Jeffie gave Juliet a sidelong smirk. "'Course, you could just drop me in town. I'll figure something out to do all day while you're at work."

Jolted from her reverie, Juliet snorted. "Why don't I just deliver you to Sheriff Blake and be done with it?" His angry look made her wish she could swallow her words. Other than Sam, nobody had ever believed in her. She should show Jeffie she believed in him rather than expecting the worst from him like everybody else.

She pulled away from the curb and headed toward the high school two blocks away. "I'm sorry."

"Yeah, right."

"So, what's your first class today?"

He huffed. "Like you care."

"Actually, I do." She slowed the truck and pulled into line with other people dropping off their kids. "We might not have grown up together, but we're probably good at some of the same subjects." When he didn't show even a flicker of interest, she sighed. "Okay, so you know which bus to take out to the ranch after school, right?"

"Duh. I'm not five." He grabbed his backpack. "Stop here." He opened the door even though they were half a block from the entrance.

"See you later, and—"

He slammed the door and was gone before she could finish her sentence. At least he headed toward the gray brick building, not away from the school. But one look at the two scruffy boys he met up with shot down any good feelings about this day. If she didn't have to get to work, she'd park and go inside to talk to the principal. Maybe later. Or maybe Sam could do that.

What was she thinking? Sam was a reluctant partner in this project, so she wouldn't bother him unless it was absolutely necessary. Besides, Jeffie was her responsibility, no matter what the judge said about sharing it with Sam.

She parked behind Billings' Burgers and entered the back door. "Hey, Jorge," she called over the pass-through to the restaurant owner, who was arranging chairs in the dining room.

"*Hola*, Juliet." The graying, sixtysomething man grinned. "Ready to do prep?"

"Sure am." She tied on a white apron, then washed her

hands. At the main worktable, she sorted through the early morning delivery of produce, starting with the onions. "Hey, Jorge, these onions smell a little off."

He came to her side and took a whiff. "You sure? They smell okay to me."

"Ya think?" She glanced at his thick-lensed bifocals. Was his sense of smell as weak as his vision? She didn't like to cross her new boss, but serving bad food could make people sick. "You know, last year there was a pretty bad outbreak of listeria in this area. A couple of people died, and lots more ended up in the hospital. They tracked it to onions." She wouldn't mention what she'd learned in chemistry class unless he insisted on using these without taking precautions to eliminate any possible deadly bacteria.

"Aw, you sound like my wife. Always worried about nothing." He shuffled toward the freezer. "Just chop the onions."

Instead, Juliet poured white vinegar and water into a large basin and added the onions. As her chemistry books advised, she'd give them a good three-minute soak that should get rid of any possible problems. She spent the rest of the morning furtively double-checking everything Jorge did.

Milly, the other waitress, arrived before the restaurant opened at eleven, and soon the busyness of serving and cleaning up dominated Juliet's thoughts. Still, every time the wall phone rang, she prayed it wasn't the high school calling about Jeffie. Silly, because of course they'd call her cell phone if he'd caused a problem. But she'd spent most of her life feeling on edge because of her family. Mama kept saying she had a new family now, the family of God. But living in the midst of people who'd looked down on the

Sizemores for well over a hundred years made it hard to feel the benefits of her new spiritual reality. She hoped— *prayed*—that people at church would open their arms to her brother as they had begun to do for her.

Sam parked on the side road leading to Petra's ranch to wait for Jeff's school bus. With Will back in town and starting to interview applicants for their newly vacant paralegal position, Sam was free to drive out here to make sure Jeff arrived home as per Judge Mathis's orders. But the yellow bus whizzed past him just as his phone buzzed. Seeing his cousin's caller ID, he punched the touchscreen on the dash.

"Rand, what's up?"

"Sorry to bother you, Cuz, but we have a situation." Rand owned Riverton's largest garden and hardware store, so Sam had a bad feeling about what that situation might be.

"Go on."

Rand cleared his throat. "Jeff Sizemore and a couple of his friends came in the store after school. Jeff made a big deal out of explaining his new living arrangement with his sister and Miss Petra. While he was waxing eloquent on the subject of you being one of his guardians, his friends were stuffing their backpacks with merchandise."

Sam's gut threatened nausea. He'd never imagined Jeff would use the Mattson name to get out of trouble, as he himself had done so many times as a teen. "Rand, I'm really sorry. I'll be right there." He checked for traffic before pulling out onto the highway.

"Good." Rand paused. "And just so you're prepared, I called Rex Blake, so he's here waiting for you and Miss Juliet."

His cousin and the sheriff were giving Jeff and his friends a bigger break than they deserved by not jailing them right away. Now Sam had to sort it out. Should he use tough love, as his parents had with him? He didn't know the other boys, but so far Jeff didn't have a record. How would he respond to strict rules?

Lord, please give me wisdom.

At the hardware store, he pulled into the parking spot beside Juliet's old Chevy and saw Sassy bent over a book in the front seat. For the briefest moment, Sam had the urge to let Rex lock the boy up for making his sister's life so complicated, not to mention his bad influence on his cute little niece. But maybe Juliet's being here was an answer to his prayer. She knew Jeff, sort of, anyway. Between them, maybe they could come up with a method for changing the boy's attitude.

Or not. As he entered the store, a female wildcat was reaming out a sullen cub in the middle of the main aisle. Sam could almost laugh, seeing Juliet's five-foot-four-inch figure raised up on tiptoes so she was nose-to-nose with her taller younger brother. Somehow Sam managed to keep a straight face. Not that anybody was looking in his direction.

"You promised to stay out of trouble, and now you're acting as a decoy for your thieving friends." She ran a hand through her blond hair and turned away, now facing Sam.

"Good. You're here. Will you say something to this… this…brother of mine?"

Sam glanced at Rex and Rand, who stood off to one side with the other boys. Rand lifted his chin in a silent greeting.

"Good to see you, Sam," Rex said. "I was about to haul these three down to the jail, but since I'll just be calling their parents or guardians to come get them, I can turn Jeff over to you and Miss Juliet."

"Okay." Sam gave Rand an apologetic frown. "Did you get everything they took?"

"I think so." Rand indicated the pile of locks, mini tool-kits, candy and other small items on the checkout counter. "I won't know for sure until I do inventory at the end of the week."

"That's all there is," one boy said.

"Shut up, stupid." The other boy punched him. "I didn't take nothing."

Hmm. Maybe the first boy was redeemable. One changed friend could turn into a better influence for Jeff.

"Okay, let's go, Jeff." Sam stepped over to him. "You ride with me." He glanced at Juliet. "That okay with you?"

"Absolutely." Her blue eyes blazing with anger, she marched toward the door, then stopped. "Mr. Mattson, I'll gladly pay for any shortfall you have in the inventory."

"Hey, I didn't take anything." Jeff posted his hands on his hips. "I was just shooting the breeze with ol' Rand, here."

Rand snorted. "I'll let you know, Miss Juliet." He glowered at Jeff. "You come into my store again, and I'll have you charged with trespassing. That goes for all three of you."

As Sam herded brother and sister from the store, he recalled both the sheriff and his cousin had addressed Juliet with southern courtesy. From the softening in her expression, he could see she'd noticed, too. Somehow that warmed his heart in the midst of this difficult situation.

Jeff reached for the door handle of Juliet's pickup.

"No. You're going with Sam." She glared at him, not giving him a choice.

Jeff didn't seem to care one way or the other and climbed into Sam's ride, although Sam could see in the boy's eyes a flicker of admiration for the complicated digital instrument cluster on the dash. But as they drove west toward the Murphy ranch, Jeff stared out the passenger window, his shoulders hunched like he expected to be hit. In his own mischievous childhood, Sam had been paddled a few times, with varying results—sometimes inciting more rebellion. From what Juliet had told him, Miss Petra often wrote about seeing Jeff around town with a black eye or bruised arm. Since Dill had sometimes slapped her around when she was growing up, it didn't take much to deduce their dad had beat up on Jeff, too, no matter how hard the kid tried to please him. That wasn't going to happen on Sam's watch, but he would have to figure out some reasonable and effective discipline. Maybe it was best to get him talking.

"So, what do you have to say for yourself?"

Jeff shot him a withering look, then turned his gaze back to the window.

"Look, Jeff, you're going to have to talk to me."

"Who says?"

Sam cleared his throat. He hated to use threats. Sometimes that caused a rebellious kid to clam up *or* deliberately defy the rules. "Judge Mathis."

Jeff winced. "Look, I didn't know Ethan and Dack were gonna steal stuff—"

"No? Then why did you strike up a conversation with Rand? It's not like you have a habit of talking with adults." Especially Mattson adults.

"I just…" He stopped and stared out the window again.

"Right."

Following some fifty yards behind Juliet's forty-year-old green Chevy Silverado, Sam weighed his next words. "Listen, Jeff—"

He ground out a tortured groan. "Like I have a choice."

Sam paused, then continued as though Jeff hadn't interrupted. "Here's the bottom line. You need to quit hanging out with those dudes and find some new friends."

"Or what?"

"Or you could end up in juvie."

When Jeff's shoulders hunched defensively, Sam stopped short of adding *like your father back in his high school days*. No need to add salt to the wound.

Ahead of them, a piece of tire suddenly shot from beneath Juliet's truck, which swerved back and forth wildly for a moment, finally screeching to a stop in the dirty snowbank on the side of the highway. Barely registering Jeff's startled exclamation, Sam slammed on the brakes, his heart in his throat, and pulled in behind her on the shoulder. Both he and Jeff jumped out of the Lariat and raced to the pickup's driver side.

"You okay?" Sam studied Juliet's pale face and widened eyes. Beside her, Sassy looked just as frightened.

"Hey, Jules, some driving." Jeff's teasing words didn't entirely disguise the tremor in his voice. Worried about his sister? That was a good sign.

"I think my tire blew." Her voice also sounded a bit shaky.

"Ya think?" Sam quipped. Now that his own heart rate had slowed a bit, he decided teasing might help these females more than showing his own fear—make that *concern*—for them. "You got a spare?" He doubted his Lariat's oversize spare would fit this forty-year-old model.

She shook her head. "I don't know. Maybe. I'll check…"

"We can do this." Sam nudged Jeff. "Let's get that tire changed."

"Me?" Jeff snorted, his usual response. "I ain't changing no stinking tire."

Sam stared at him briefly. "You're fifteen, and you don't know how to change a tire?"

"Didn't say I didn't know—"

Sam guessed Dill hadn't bothered to teach his son basic survival skills. "So you haven't taken shop class yet?"

"Shop? No way. I'm into computers. Brain work, not dirty jobs."

"Well, kid, it's time to get those hands dirty." He gripped Jeff's shoulder lightly and directed him to the back of the Chevy. To his relief, a full-size spare was attached to the rack under the truck bed. It would require some air, so he fetched his portable tire inflator from his ride and instructed Jeff in how to use it. To his surprise, Jeff's hands shook as he tried to remove the valve cap and still shook as he struggled to insert the compressor nozzle into the valve. Was this a motor skill problem, the forty-degree weather or just more rebellion? He kept glancing over his shoulder at Sam as if…what? Sam had seen enough abused kids to figure it out. Jeff was scared to mess up. Scared he'd be hit.

"You can do it, Uncle Jeffie." Sassy appeared around the back of the Chevy, all traces of her fear gone.

Sam could see a slight softening in the boy's expression. "Hear that, Jeff? Your niece believes in you, and so do I. Just take a deep breath and concentrate."

Jeff huffed, clenched his jaw and gave a quick nod, as though determined to conquer this job. This was good. Maybe he hadn't succeeded at many things in his short life. Sam remembered how every achievement had brought praise from his parents and boosted his own self-confidence. It would be gratifying to help Jeff do the same.

Watching Sam guide Jeffie in changing the tire, Juliet worked hard to quiet her shaken nerves. Thank the Lord she'd managed to avoid flipping the truck on the soft shoulder despite going close to seventy when the tire blew. Even without the flat tire, Mama's old truck shouldn't be driven so fast.

Once Jeff had the spare inflated, he reached for the jack.

"Hang on," Sam said. "We need to loosen the lug nuts first so the weight of the truck keeps the wheel from spinning." He handed Jeffie the lug wrench. "Here you go."

Jeffie took several seconds to attach the wrench, then couldn't budge the nut.

"Let me help—" Sam reached out.

"I can do it!" Jeffie put his whole body into forcing the wrench to turn. When it finally loosened, the other three came off more easily. He refused Sam's help with the jack and took obvious pride in raising the truck several inches off the ground.

For the first time since Juliet returned to Riverton and reconnected with her brother, she saw a softening in his face, almost like he was eager to learn and perform this skill. Sam's obvious patience was a far cry from her father's rough demands, always giving orders but never showing his kids how to do anything. From Juliet's teenage interactions with Brenda, she guessed the woman spent most of her marriage to Dad in a state of justifiable fear. She'd loved Jeffie, but she'd pushed him to behave so he'd please Dill, which only incited more rebellion in the boy. Juliet couldn't pass judgment on their unhappy household. Even Mama hadn't been the most patient parent to Juliet.

Now that she was a Christian, she seemed to have found peace that brought with it a more patient nature.

The spare tire in place, Sam double-checked the lug nuts. The truck lacked hubcaps, so they were finished. "Good job, kid."

To Juliet's surprise, Jeffie didn't bristle at being called "kid."

"You did it, Jeffie." Sassy hopped around and clapped her hands.

Sam caught Sassy's gaze and winked, then turned his eyes toward Juliet...and frowned.

"Let's get going," he said, his voice oddly gruff. "Miss Petra will be worried."

"I texted her." Juliet waved Sassy back into the truck. "We'll meet you there."

Supper was almost ready, and Sam accepted Mama's invitation to eat with them. The round kitchen table wouldn't hold everybody, so Juliet and Sassy set the oblong dining room table while Raeder, Jeffie and Peanut took care of the milking.

Texting on his phone, Sam leaned against the doorjamb between kitchen and dining room, phone in hand. "Miss Petra, you're mighty brave to take on helping us with Jeff."

Mama smiled as she ladled green beans into a serving bowl. "Glad to do it. That boy's had a rough time of it his whole life. Maybe we can remedy some of that." She swiped the back of her hand across her forehead. "One thing's sure. He needs the Lord. Needs to know God's a good, good Father. Not mean and angry like ol' Dill."

"Yes, ma'am." Sam glanced at Juliet and shrugged an apology.

Was he apologizing because he agreed with Mama or because he'd accepted the invitation to supper? She still couldn't read him like she had in high school. Back then, they completed each other's sentences and shared laughs over the same things. An ache opened in her heart. She'd never had a friend like Sam before or since those days. Despite loving him, like every other girl she'd ever known, she'd desperately wanted to please her father, too. Yet what had that brought her but grief and the eventual realization that Dad only wanted to hurt anybody named Mattson, specifically by depriving Sam of his child?

If only she could go back in time…no, Mama told her that kind of thinking wasn't helpful. The only way forward for both her and Sassy was to trust the Lord and look to the future. A future that would undoubtedly involve Sam's eventual discovery that Sassy was his daughter. Which would only solidify his obvious dislike and distrust of Juliet. Although she'd long ago given up on her teenage love for him, somehow that saddened her more than words could express.

Sam pocketed his phone and crossed his arms. "Will it be convenient for you if I take Jeff out to Double Bar M this Saturday to choose a calf for his 4-H project?"

Juliet stared at him for a moment. "Yeah. Sure. I forgot about that."

"Mom, can I have a calf for 4-H, too?" Sassy gave Juliet her winning smile that usually earned her whatever she asked for. "I'll take real good care of it."

Juliet exchanged a questioning look with Sam, and a pleasant little hiccup bounced around in her chest. This was the way they used to communicate. "Um, well—"

"I've got an idea." Sam gave Sassy a friendly smile, as he would to any child. "What would you think of raising chickens for your project?"

Mama appeared in the dining room doorway, a milk

pitcher in hand. "That's a great idea. We always need eggs, but I don't have time for chickens." She set the pitcher on the table, then gave Sassy a side hug. "Chickens would be an important addition to our little ranch."

Juliet's heart warmed, and she shot a grateful grin at Mama. "What do you think, Sass?"

Rather than sulking over not getting her way, as Jeffie would, Sassy scrunched up her forehead thoughtfully. "Well, since Gramma needs eggs… Can I still wear cowboy boots?"

"Sure," Sam said. "You'll need 'em stomping around the barnyard. Right, Mom?" He winked at Juliet, and another hiccup bounced in her chest. "I'll check with Raeder and we'll figure out what we need for a chicken coop."

Baby chickens, feed, boots, a coop…how could Juliet afford all this stuff on her uncertain salary at the burger joint? But one look at Sassy's joyful expression was reason enough to shove those worries aside. Somehow they would manage, no matter what she had to give up for herself.

Chapter Five

As Sam drove home in the dark with a sprinkle of snow bouncing off his windshield, he muttered to himself. What was wrong with him, offering to help Sassy with her 4-H project? Being roped into helping Jeff already ate at his gut. For well over a hundred and forty years, the Sizemores had made it their mission to do all the harm they could to the Mattson clan, so Sam felt like a traitor. In high school, he'd deliberately taken up with the "enemy," and look where that had gotten him. Now he was stuck helping the girl…woman who'd broken his heart as a result of his rebellion. How could he tackle the problem he'd created for himself?

He didn't regret suggesting Jeff should join 4-H, but did this mean he'd have to take the boy to meetings? Did Juliet realize she needed to enroll both kids through the extension office as soon as possible? Who would help them keep up their record books that tracked their projects and public service activities?

Then there was the matter of dues. Could Juliet afford to pay for them? Judge Mathis hadn't indicated that Sam had any financial responsibility for Jeff, and he sure wasn't responsible for Sassy's needs. Maybe if he could find out who her birth father was, he could go after the guy for support. That thought didn't settle well in his mind, but he shoved away his doubts. New Mexico law didn't look kindly on deadbeat dads, and more than once, Sam had sent the courts after men who didn't step up to their responsibilities. On the other hand, he doubted Juliet would voluntarily give up the name of the man she'd cheated with, and Sam wasn't about to ask her. For his spiritual health, one of these days he would have to forgive her for that betrayal, but right now he wasn't quite ready.

All of these ruminations didn't solve the immediate situation. Both Sassy and Jeff needed to join 4-H for their own good. The organization taught kids valuable lessons. Most Mattson kids joined as five-year-old Cloverbuds and aged out at eighteen with a passel of ribbons and awards. What else could Sam help them with while still keeping hold of his own heart?

He'd made a start after Miss Petra's fantastic chili-flavored meatloaf supper. He and Raeder had scoured the ranch for usable materials for the chicken coop. They found boards—and a few frozen snakes—in the snow-encrusted lumber pile beside the main barn. In the once-cluttered, chaotic workshop that Raeder had cleaned up and organized, they found nails and some chicken wire, but more would be needed to keep out predators. They'd have to wire electricity into the coop to be sure the baby chicks and possibly some laying hens could survive the rest of the winter, which sometimes lasted into May. Lots of work, but Sam welcomed any kind of hands-on labor to give him some much-needed exercise.

At work the next day, Will announced he'd hired their new office assistant, their cousin Livvy Mattson. "She's a sophomore at Riverton Community College and majoring in business with an eye to becoming a paralegal. She can start next Monday."

"That sure does simplify things." Sam chuckled. "Not that we're guilty of nepotism or anything. Did you interview any other applicants?"

"A couple of high school girls, but none were qualified. Hey, cuz, I know the law. Besides, we've watched her grow up, so we know she's hardworking and reliable. Plus I asked Lauren to give her the office tour, and she gave Livvy a thumbs-up."

"Ah. That's all I needed to hear." Sam headed toward his office. "Thanks for doing the heavy lifting on this."

He settled in his desk chair and reached for the file containing his next case. This adoption should be easy to complete because the newlywed husband was eager to be a dad to his bride's three kids. Unlike Rob and Lauren's situation last fall, no one would contest this adoption. If only every family complication resolved as easily, life would be much simpler.

As he read this man's letter stating his desire to raise these kids as his own, Sam's eyes burned. He didn't usually get emotionally involved with his clients' lives. But he couldn't help pondering the contrast between a good man stepping up to be a father to someone else's kids and a degenerate like Dill Sizemore who killed his wife and left his own son a virtual orphan. Unlike Sam, Jeff had no idea what it was like to have a loving father. As Petra said, the boy needed to know God is a good, good Father. And little Sassy needed to know that, too.

But surely the Lord didn't want Sam to be responsible for making up for that deficit in the lives of these two kids. Did He?

* * *

Juliet didn't know how much longer she could keep saving Jorge from disaster without him knowing what she'd done. Today it was wood chips from the ancient chopping board mingling with the lettuce. She managed to toss the veggies and the board, then chop up more lettuce before Jorge noticed what she was doing. He wasn't out to hurt anybody. In fact, he often handed out free burgers to homeless folks needing a hot meal on these bitter winter days. Yet despite several health department warning citations and a one-month closure before Juliet was hired, he didn't seem aware of the finer points of kitchen cleanliness. And she couldn't say anything to Milly because the girl was related to Jorge.

At the end of her lunch shift and beyond her quitting time, she scrubbed the prep table, the grill and every other food area, mopped the floor with disinfecting cleaner and started the dishwasher. What the evening crew did with the kitchen was up to them, but she took selfies with the clean kitchen as proof that she'd done her duty. With her earned reputation of being less than truthful, she wanted to prove she'd changed her life for the better.

After picking Sassy up at school, she made a grocery run for Mama, then headed home…and got stuck behind the school bus on the two-lane highway. Of course it stopped every hundred yards, letting off students at various crossroads and entrances to subdivisions, so it—not to mention the cloud of exhaust it emitted—was impossible to pass. Lost in thought, it took her a while to realize Sassy wasn't her usual chatty self. In fact, at the grocery store she hadn't asked for any treats as she usually did.

"Hey, baby, how was your day? Sorry I didn't ask sooner."

Sassy shrugged. "It was okay." No bright smile accompanied her words.

A sick feeling stirred in Juliet's stomach. She couldn't let a bad situation fester in her precious child. "What happened?"

Fat tears tracked down Sassy's sun-kissed cheeks. "Mommy, did my granddaddy kill Jeffie's mommy?" She only called Juliet "Mommy" when she felt vulnerable.

Juliet tamped down her persistent anger at Dad. Murdering Brenda had been the tragic capstone of a life of bad choices. "Sweetheart, who told you that?"

"Ginny Gray." Sassy sniffed. "She sits behind me and got mad when I wouldn't give her my math answers."

Juliet's anger shifted to this unknown child. Kids could be so cruel. "I'm proud of you for not sharing your work with her. She needs to learn math for herself." That wasn't all that brat needed to learn, but Juliet wouldn't let herself give vent to such thoughts.

"Is it true? About my granddaddy?"

The plaintive sound in Sassy's usually cheerful voice broke Juliet's heart. She inhaled a deep breath and let it out slowly, then sent up a silent prayer not to pass on her anger to her daughter.

"Remember what the minister said on Sunday? We've all sinned and fallen short of what God wants us to do." She glanced at Sassy, then back at the road, making sure not to come too close to the school bus. "Remember?"

"Uh-huh."

"So we're all sinners, and we need Jesus, right?"

"Uh-huh." Sassy's forehead scrunched up as it did when she was puzzling over a matter. "But me and you never killed nobody."

Juliet would hold off on the grammar lesson for now.

"No, but sin is sin." She sent up another prayer. "Some sins hurt people more than others, but they're still sin." Sins such as lying about Sam's paralegal, now his cousin's new wife. Sam had looked pretty skeptical when she'd confessed it to him, but maybe she could improve his opinion of her over time. She didn't want his distrust of her to interfere with his helping Jeffie.

"So cheating at math is bad, but not as bad as killing somebody?" A glance revealed Sassy's expression had softened.

"Well…" This little girl sure did test her mama. "To answer your first question, yes, Jeffie's and my dad did—" she had no way of softening the words or the deed "—did kill Brenda, Jeffie's mother. He was—" No, she would not make the excuse that Dill had probably been drunk.

"Poor Brenda." Sassy sniffed. "Poor Jeffie. Now he doesn't have a mom." She reached over to set a hand on Juliet's forearm. "I'm so glad I still have my mom."

"Me, too, baby." Juliet swallowed a sob. "Me, too."

"And, Mom?" Some of her old sass crept back into her voice.

"Yes?"

"Next time we drive home after school—" she waved a hand in front of her face "—can we not follow the stinky old school bus?"

Juliet snorted out a laugh. "I'll try."

Ahead, the bus stopped at the road to Mama's ranch, and Jeff emerged, his backpack over his shoulder. For the first time, Juliet noticed he wore a jean jacket. Didn't he have a winter coat?

She turned down the lane and stopped. "Hop aboard, little brother." She offered a smile.

He didn't return one, just climbed in the truck beside Sassy. "Move over, Squirt."

Sassy giggled. "Say please."

"You wish. Move it." Despite his choice of words, his tone was as soft as always when he spoke to Sassy.

Once they were headed down the two-hundred-yard lane, Sassy snuggled under Jeffie's arm. "Did you have a good day?"

"What's it to you?" He tweaked her nose.

Giggling again, she batted away his hand. "Just hoping yours was better than mine."

"You need me to beat somebody up?"

"Hey. None of that." Juliet glared briefly at her brother. "You getting in trouble again is the last thing we need."

He scoffed, then pulled Sassy closer. "It's us against them, kid. We Sizemores gotta stick together."

How well Juliet remembered their father touting that same idea. Yet he'd lived for himself without regard for what his choices would do to his kids.

She glanced in the rearview mirror and saw Sam following behind them. When she'd stopped behind the bus, her attention had been on Jeffie, so she'd barely registered Sam's fancy blue truck on the side of the road. Like clockwork, he was checking up on Jeffie. In one way, she was relieved to have his masculine influence on her brother. In another, she resented having him look over her shoulder to be sure she was raising Jeffie the right way. But she also couldn't stop the tug on her heart over what might have been if only she'd managed to escape her father and elope with Sam all those years ago.

Forgetting those things that are behind, Saint Paul had written to the Philippian church two millennia ago. For

Juliet, right here and right now, that was easier said than done when her past was in front of her face every moment of every day.

Sam pulled in beside Juliet as the kids were spilling out of the pickup door, shoving and teasing like siblings. This was good. Jeff's big-brotherly treatment of his niece was a promising sign, hopefully indicative of some decency in his character, as was his interest in raising a steer. Sam planned to look for more ways to tap into those better qualities.

Wearing pink earmuffs, her cheeks rosy from the cold, Juliet walked around the front of her truck and waved. His heart dipped. Why did she have to look so pretty? He returned a wave, then hooked a thumb over his shoulder toward the back of his truck. She'd already turned toward the house, so she missed seeing what he'd brought. Raeder had texted him a list of items they needed for the chicken coop, including three rolls of half-inch chicken wire, a bundle of stakes and various hardware. Sam bought them at Rand's store earlier this afternoon.

In one way, he felt a little excited about this project. In his job, he often worked with families and helped lots of kids in difficult situations. But this was the first time he would be working personally with two of them. Too bad it also meant he had to be around Juliet. At least his bitterness was beginning to fade. He'd seen too many single moms struggle to survive to be immune to their plights, even Juliet's. On the other hand, he still wasn't ready to forgive her for having a child with another man and breaking her promise to elope with Sam. But he was determined to rein in his hurt even though he had to see her every day.

He climbed out of the truck. "Hey, Jeff. Give me a hand with this load."

Jeff turned around, as did Juliet and Sassy. "Say please." He smirked at Sassy like they had a secret. She giggled.

Sam chuckled. "Please."

"Here, Squirt." Jeff handed his backpack to Sassy. "Put this in my room."

The weight of the bag made her step back and catch her balance, but she managed not to drop it. "Say please."

He ruffled her hair. "Puh-leez."

Their teasing stirred up good memories of Sam's relationship with his younger sister. While he'd been Sadie's protector, she'd been a sounding board for him when he rebelled against their parents. Maybe he could tap into those memories for ways to encourage Jeff.

While Juliet and Sassy headed toward the house, Jeff ambled over to the truck and eyed the rolls of wire. "What's this for?"

"A chicken yard for Sassy's chickens." Even as he said the girl's name, sadness nearly choked him. Where was her father? *Who* was he? Did he still live around here? *Stop it!* Trying to guess was useless speculation, and he sure wouldn't ask Juliet for the man's name.

"You bought it for Sassy?" The doubt in Jeff's voice brought Sam back to the project at hand.

"Yeah, well." He chuckled. "I'll expect free eggs for a year."

Jeff snorted. "Right."

They each carried a roll toward the barn, where Raeder and Peanut met them.

"Hey, guys." Raeder tilted his hat back. "Looks like you got the right stuff. I laid out the yard like we discussed and tried digging post holes. Ground's frozen, so we'll have to put that off a bit. Did you decide about ordering one of those coop kits?"

"I did. It should arrive next Tuesday." Sam set his roll of wire on the ground beside the barn door.

"What should arrive by Tuesday?" Juliet approached them, to Sam's surprise.

"Sam's buying Sassy a chicken coop." Jeff seemed in a hurry to announce the news.

"What?" Juliet put her fists at her waist. "What gives you the right…" She stopped and stared down at her feet for a moment before glaring up at Sam. "Look, Judge Mathis said you were to help me with Jeff, but that doesn't give you the right—" she paused and bit her lower lip "—I mean, the responsibility to do anything for my daughter." She shot a cross look at her brother and pointed to the roll of wire beside him. "Put that back in Sam's truck."

"Aw, come on, Sis." Jeff mirrored her posture, fists at his waist. "Let him buy stuff for her. The Mattsons owe us—"

"No!" Her eyes widened with what almost seemed like fear. "Nobody owes us anything. When will you get that through your head?"

Despite her being several inches shorter than her brother, he cringed. Then sulked.

Lord, help me out here. Please. Sam cleared his throat and traded a look with Raeder, who nodded. They'd talked about this.

"Miss Juliet," Raeder said, "I was hoping Sassy and Peanut could do the chicken thing together. He's almost old enough to be a 4-H Cloverbud, so it would be a real fine project for him. Would that be okay with you?"

Juliet looked between Raeder and Sam and sighed. "I already agreed to the project for Sassy. It's the expense of all this stuff that's a problem. I have to budget for it, and right now I don't have the money."

"Listen, Sis." Jeff punched her arm lightly. "Ol' Sam here says we can pay him back in eggs. Whaddaya think of that?"

Juliet blinked in the cutest way, so cute Sam had to turn away. "Chickens and eggs. Right." She huffed out a dramatic sigh. "Well, in that case…" She shrugged. "Okay." Another glance at Sam revealed her eyes had reddened. "Thanks."

He tried not to smile but failed. "You're welcome. Now can we just get on with these projects and not quibble about the details? We want these kids to succeed in 4-H, right?"

"Right." She huffed out another big sigh and turned to walk back to the house.

Clearly she didn't like this situation any more than Sam did. Never mind that it was her fault they were stuck together with a glue named Jeff. If she hadn't come to him last week and asked for help…

No matter how he tried not to let his feelings get in the way, he had to be honest with himself. Against all reason, he was glad she'd come to him.

Chapter Six

When Sam gave her that devastating Mattson grin, Juliet had to turn away because her pulse had kicked up real bad. Why did he have to be so incredibly handsome? But letting him spend money on Sassy, even if Peanut was part of the plan, was dangerous. What was she thinking? No matter how hard she tried to control the situation, he was going to find out Sassy was his daughter.

First he'd be angry. Then he'd feel obliged to provide for her. *Then* all the other Mattsons would accuse her of trapping him so she could get her hands on a share of that Mattson wealth. Gossip would run rampant, and life for her would become unlivable here in Riverton. Maybe these were all stupid imaginings, because if she really was after Mattson money, she'd have told him about Sassy long ago.

Never once in their school days had she ever coveted anything that family owned. Never once had she sought Sam out or tried to trap him. He'd been the one to chase her, probably because dating a Sizemore was the most rebellious thing a Mattson could do in their small town.

She would never forget that cold winter day in eighth grade when she'd endured yet another verbal assault from the mean girls about her family's so-called "cattle rustling" reputation. Sam had brought his tray over to the table where she sat alone, as always, and plopped down across from her.

"Mind if I join you?" He'd flashed that smile, and right away she'd been lost in it.

Somehow she'd managed to shrug. "Your choice."

"You look like you've been crying." The kindness in his voice had brought more tears.

"What's it to you?" She'd pushed against the table to stand and leave, but he'd touched her hand.

"Juliet, right?" As if everybody didn't know her name. "Look, you don't have to listen to those dumb girls."

"*Ha.* You don't if your name is Mattson." She'd settled back in her chair as a strangely pleasant sensation began to wind through her chest. "Mine being Sizemore, it's a little different. Everybody assumes the worst about me."

"Yeah, well." He'd snorted out a laugh. "Try living up to the reputations of generations of perfect Mattson men, superhero ranchers one and all." He'd rolled those blue-green eyes. "Y'know what? Soon as I graduate, I'm gonna ditch this place and go where nobody's ever heard the name Mattson."

Juliet remembered laughing, then saying the words that sealed her future. "Sounds like a plan. Take me with you?"

He'd winked at her and flashed that killer Mattson smile again. "You got it, Jules."

They'd been inseparable from that day on, until…

"You're awful quiet, honey." Mama brought Juliet back to the present as she dished up the mashed potatoes and handed her the bowl. "Did work go okay?"

"Just the usual." Juliet carried the bowl to the dining room table to avoid saying more. If she told Mama what she'd been thinking and feeling, Mama would again urge her to tell Sam the truth now. If the thought didn't make her sick to her stomach, she'd do it just to get Mama off her back. Sure, it hurt like crazy for Sam to assume she'd been unfaithful to him. She'd seen the pain in those blue-green eyes last week as he calculated Sassy's age compared to when they'd been intimate. Hot shame flooded her cheeks as she recalled the sin that resulted in her pregnancy. But God had given beauty for ashes when He created Sassy.

Raeder came in from milking and set a steaming, froth-topped bucket on the table in the small mudroom right outside the kitchen. Behind him, Jeff brought the second bucket, and behind him, Peanut carried a pint-size, half-full pail. Raeder sure was doing a good job of parenting his little cowboy, even helping Peanut pour his milk through cheesecloth into a clean gallon jar, as he and Jeff had done with the larger buckets. Raeder placed the strained gallons of milk in the old refrigerator on the back porch, where Mama's customers could pick up their milk and put their payments in a jar on the table. Everyone operated on the honor system, and the money helped Mama with other expenses.

"Where's Sam?" Mama glanced toward the door, then continued to fork ham slices from the cast-iron skillet onto a platter.

"Said he had to get home and do his own milking." Raeder washed his hands in the mudroom sink, then helped Peanut do the same.

Unreasonable disappointment filled Juliet's heart. What was wrong with her? Maybe she was just annoyed because she'd expected to discuss tomorrow's trip to his family's ranch to choose a steer for Jeff. Had her attitude about the chickens driven him away?

As Mama called everybody to the table, Juliet's phone dinged. She pulled it from her pocket and read Sam's cryptic text, Ten tomorrow DBMR. DBMR, the acronym for the Mattsons' Double Bar M Ranch. She returned a thumbs-up emoji, even as her appetite plummeted.

She needed Sam's assurance that none of his family would be rude to her brother. Not that Jeff didn't deserve a cold shoulder after the way he'd threatened to trip Sam's new Cousin Zoey at the homecoming dance last fall. But after he'd seen his mother murdered by their father, Juliet had noticed a change in him, even if no one else had. Then there was his brotherly behavior toward Sassy and little Peanut. If only Juliet could shout it out to the entire community. But like her, Jeff would have to prove to everybody that he'd changed. Easier said than done in a community that had hated their family for well over a hundred years.

Trying to redeem her family's reputation weighed heavy on her shoulders, but she didn't dare, much less want to, try to shrug it off.

"Take a look and tell me what you see." Sam waved a hand toward the Angus herd milling around the north pasture, their breath blowing out in puffy white streams.

Shoulders already hunched to brace against the stiff winter breeze, Jeff managed a shrug. "A bunch of black cows. Big cows. Little cows. Medium cows." He shrugged again.

Or was that a shiver? The kid really needed something warmer than a jean jacket, but Sam doubted Juliet would let him buy a coat for Jeff. Right now, she was focused on the ranch's main abode, affectionately called the Big House by the family, a frown darkening her brow. No need for her to worry. However reluctantly, Rob had agreed to let Jeff choose a calf.

"What do you think, Jules... Juliet?" *Ack!* Why had

he used the fond nickname he'd given her back in school? That fondness had been replaced by an icy lump where his heart used to be. He didn't dare let it thaw, not when she'd cheated on him and had another man's baby.

She turned her attention to her brother. "No, I want Jeffie to figure this out. I'm just the driver today."

"Good plan." Sam rested his arms on the fence's top rail. "Okay, Jeff, it's important to know what you're looking for. Notice that one?" He pointed to a frisky little calf romping away from its mother and back again. "He's a little bigger than the others around his age, the ones born since Christmas. That's one thing to look for. His back is straight. That's important. Now watch as he runs how his back feet land in the same spot as his front feet. That shows soundness." Eyes narrowed, Jeff mirrored Sam's posture, resting his arms on the fence, and stared at the calf, so Sam continued. "His stride is long, and from the way he wiggles around, you can see his skeleton is flexible."

Jeff nodded. "Can I pet him?"

Sam chuckled. "Sure." He opened the gate and ushered Jeff through, with Juliet following behind them. "Just relax and walk normally. Cows can get spooked easily, especially when they have calves."

He guided Jeff to the calf and halted its romping. "Easy, little fella. Let's take a look at you." He ran a gloved hand down its side. "It's a little early to tell how he'll develop, but all the signs are good." He pointed to the shoulders, rump and ribs. "These will fatten up if you give him the right feed and minerals."

Jeff glanced at Juliet. "You gonna buy that stuff for me?"

Her bright blue eyes widened. "Me? I can't afford to buy cattle feed, much less cattle vitamins." She traded a look with Sam. "But we can find you a job so you can earn the money."

A pinch of respect spiked in Sam's chest. Then concern. What did she mean by *we*?

"A job? What about school? If I have a job, how am I supposed to do that homework you said is so important?"

"You'll manage." Juliet smirked. "It's a rite of passage for every self-respecting person on their journey to adulthood."

Jeff rolled his eyes, then stroked the calf's head like he was petting a dog. Sam noted that he didn't wear gloves, and his hands were red from the cold. "So he needs to get fat so he can be a strong bull and make lots of baby calves?"

Again, Sam traded a look with Juliet. This was getting to be a habit he wasn't sure was healthy, at least not for him. "Um, no. You'll be raising him to sell at market."

"Right." Juliet laughed. "Where do you think all those hamburgers come from you like so much? And that steak you had at the steakhouse?"

Stepping back from the animal and jamming his hands in his jacket pockets, Jeff gaped at his sister. "That's different. I ain't raising no calf like it's a pet just to kill it off for hamburgers."

Sam tilted his hat back from his forehead. "What exactly did you think would happen to your steer?"

"I thought I'd be raising a bull, or maybe a milk cow. You know. Like Miss Petra's Bruiser and Maude and Chloe."

If Sam wasn't mistaken, it seemed the kid's eyes turned a little red. His reluctance to nurture an animal, then eat it, could possibly reveal a tender heart. Sam needed to encourage that trait. *Lord, please give me wisdom.* "Okay. Maybe we can arrange for you to raise one of our Holstein heifers." Rob might have a fit over this change of plan, but Sam would deal with his cousin if and when that time came. For now, the half smile of relief on Jeff's face was sufficient reward for Sam to know he'd made the right decision.

As they left the pasture, Juliet looped an arm around Jeff's. "Now, about that part-time job. Got any ideas?"

"Huh. Fat chance I can get hired in this town." Jeff leaned into his sister's shoulder as they walked arm in arm. "Maybe Miss Petra will hire me—"

"Jeffie, you know she can't afford another hand. It's hard enough for her to pay Raeder a decent wage." She glanced over her shoulder at Sam. "Besides, we owe her for making a home for us without asking for rent and board."

Sam could see the pain in her eyes. She was doing her best to help Jeff, but it couldn't be easy for her. "I'll ask around. Maybe somebody needs help a couple of hours after school."

"I ain't doing no janitor work."

"You got a better idea?" Juliet scoffed. "I mean, with all your experience?"

He winced. "Yeah, well…"

One possible job came to mind, but Sam would check it out before saying anything. Jeff had already endured too much disappointment in his young life. No sense in adding to it by giving him false hope or making him apply for jobs only to face rejection.

"See you in church tomorrow." Juliet walked around her battered pickup and climbed in, while Jeff got in the near side.

Through the window, Sam could see the kid wrapping himself in a blanket. With black exhaust billowing out of the tailpipe, the pickup chugged toward the automatic gate, which opened to let them drive over the cattle grate. Didn't Juliet or Miss Petra know they needed to change the oil every three thousand miles? Maybe Sam should put a bug in Raeder's ear about that.

He blew out a long sigh. He couldn't solve all of her problems, not when he needed to talk Rob out of one of the new Holstein heifers. But he also had to follow up on a job for the kid. When he'd bought the chicken wire at the garden and hardware store, he'd noticed Rand was short-handed. Could he be persuaded to give Jeff a chance despite that shoplifting incident? Sam and Rand both had had their times of rebellion, and folks had given them second, third and sometimes fourth breaks, mainly because their name was Mattson. Would Rand grant the same kind of break to a Sizemore?

Sam hated seeing Jeff freezing in the late February wind. What kind of parents didn't buy a warm coat for their son to wear in these bitter New Mexico winters? Poor Brenda Sizemore had been a nurse's aide at the Riverton hospital, so she hadn't made much money. But Dill, when he was sober, had worked at a bar in Española. With his salary and tips, surely their combined incomes had been sufficient to meet their family's needs. But then, maybe Dill drank up most of his earnings. If the Lord ever blessed Sam with a child, he'd gladly give up every self-indulgence and even necessities to make sure that child had everything he or she needed.

An odd little thought began to grow in the back of his mind. Yep. That was a good idea. And he couldn't wait to get to town and follow through on it.

"Oh, yeah, you *are* going to church with us."

Seated at the breakfast table, Juliet tried to speak in a

calm voice, difficult to accomplish with Jeffie glaring at her, rebellion blazing from his eyes. At times like this, he looked so much like Dad, whose handsome face could turn ugly when he was in a rage. Jeffie hadn't even dressed for church despite her telling him to last night. He wore tattered jeans and a T-shirt stained with a drop of grape jelly on the front. She suspected he'd let it fall from his biscuit on purpose.

"Why do I have to go listen to that preacher tell me I'm a bad person? Everybody else is already doing that."

Oh, this kid sure did know how to push her buttons. *Lord, give me patience.*

"Jeff, we're all bad people." Mama joined them at the table with her plate of eggs, bacon and biscuits. "The Bible says we've all sinned and come short of the glory of God. That's why we need Jesus."

A mischievous grin crossed Jeffie's lips. "So when somebody tells me I'm bad, I can throw it right back in their face, right?"

"Who said you're bad?" Raeder entered the kitchen dressed for church, Peanut following behind him. Raeder served their plates from the stove and they took their usual places at the table.

"You ain't from around here, are you?" Jeff smirked, then sat up in his chair. "We Sizemores are the worst of the worst." He thrust out his chest like he was proud of that label. "Thieves. Cattle rustlers. Liars. You name it, we've done it." He snorted. "Hey, we're even murderers." His voice broke a little on that last word, and he jumped to his feet. "Seein' ol' Raeder in his Sunday best, I guess I'd better wear the same." He strode from the kitchen and pounded up the stairs.

"Sorry I asked." Raeder gave Juliet an apologetic grimace.

"I want to go to church." Sassy came close to whining. Yesterday before they left for the Mattson ranch, she'd pouted when Juliet told her she couldn't go help Jeff choose a calf. Only a promise that they would spend time on her chicken project that afternoon kept her from a tantrum, something Juliet had never dealt with. Was she jealous of Juliet's concern for Jeffie?

"Yeah, me, too, sweet pea." Juliet reached over to caress her daughter's cheek. "And before church, you can go to Sunday school."

"Awesome. I like Sunday school." She grinned as she forked up another bite of egg.

Jeffie's "Sunday best" turned out to be well-worn jeans with pantleg hems that didn't reach the tops of his sneakers and the secondhand denim shirt his foster parents had given him for Brenda's funeral. And of course, his thin jean jacket. But he'd refused to borrow her extra coat, even though it didn't look all that feminine. A battered baseball cap sat backward over his sandy-blond hair. Juliet felt sick that she hadn't been able to buy him some new clothes or even something from a thrift shop.

They all piled into Raeder's Bronco, one of the few remnants of his rodeo days when he'd been making good money. His bum leg still healing, he asked Juliet to drive. Only a couple of years old, the SUV was in good condition, thanks to Raeder's skill with all things mechanical. It was the nicest vehicle she'd ever driven.

Although Sunday morning traffic was light, the drive took almost half an hour. Finding a spot in the church parking lot, Juliet pulled in and shut off the motor.

Raeder climbed out and lifted Peanut down from his car seat. "See you guys later. Let's go, partner." The father and son headed toward the Sunday school building.

"Mama, will you please take Sassy to her class?" Juliet needed to make sure Jeffie didn't skip out on his.

"Sure. Let's go, hon." Mama opened the back passenger door and held out a hand to Sassy.

"Mommy…" Sassy whined. "I want you to take me."

"Hey." Jeffie fake-punched Sassy's arm. "Remember, if anybody gives you a problem, you let me know." He winked at her. "We Sizemores gotta stick together."

His remarks seemed to settle Sassy, but they made Juliet's stomach lurch. After Mama and Sassy walked away, she gripped Jeffie's arm.

"Listen, you need to stop saying things like that to Sassy. She didn't grow up here, so she doesn't know how people see us. Maybe they'll be kinder to her. Besides, how can we ever change their view of us if we don't accept that we have a lot to live down?"

He shrugged her off. "You ain't been listening to Sass, have you? That Ginny Gray keeps saying stuff to her when the teachers aren't looking."

Who's that brat to be so mean to Sassy? Juliet quashed her anger. At all costs, she had to keep her head even when the unexpected happened. "Look, let's don't let the behavior of other people affect our reactions. Let's find you a Sunday school class."

"Let's not." He leaned back against the Bronco, crossed his arms and rolled his eyes in his usual annoyed teenager way. She'd probably done the same to Mama when she was his age.

"Morning, you two." Sam jogged toward them looking sharp in his heavy Western-style parka, blue shirt and black bolo tie. And carrying a large Walmart bag, which he held out to Jeffie. "Here. This is for you."

Jeffie stared at the bag for a moment before taking it in

hand and pulling out a brand-new, warm-looking brown parka. The struggle on his face broke Juliet's heart. Her brother's pride, inherited from and reinforced by their father, could easily be his downfall. Despite her own reluctance to take anything from this man, she desperately wanted Jeffie to have a warm coat. *Please, Lord, let him accept it.*

"This is just a loan, okay?" Sam tilted his head toward the Bronco. "You can leave it in here if you don't want to wear it inside."

"Ha." Jeffie snorted. "And have somebody steal it? Then you'll make me pay for it."

Sam's right eyebrow shot up. "I don't think anybody would steal it here in the church parking lot."

"Ha," Jeffie repeated. "I've seen guys scoping out cars all over this town looking for something to steal."

Sam traded a look with Juliet, one that made her heart hiccup. She had to stop connecting with him this way. Was he thinking Jeff referred to himself?

"Not to worry, kid." Sam grinned. "We have deacons patrolling the parking lot."

"Figures." Jeffie snickered. "Preaching all about love but always judging us sinners." He made air quotes with that last word.

Sam gave him an understanding nod. "Well, kid, we're all sinners. Let's go find you a Sunday school class so you can learn more about that."

Despite the cold wind blowing through her four layers of clothing, Juliet's heart warmed. Sam had just reinforced Mama's mini sermon from breakfast. Maybe among the three of them, they could help Jeffie see his need for Jesus and truly turn his life around. She and Sam hadn't talked deeply about spiritual matters, but she had a feeling he'd trusted Jesus at some point in his life. While she'd never expect him to trust her again, that mutual faith in God should go a long way to help her brother. She would pray without ceasing for that to happen.

Jeffie hesitated briefly before shrugging into the coat. Even though he refused her help to get his jean jacket into the sleeves, Juliet saw this as another reason to hope that her brother's life would turn around, as hers had.

Lord, please make it so.

Chapter Seven

Sam and Juliet stood outside the Sunday school room and watched through the window in the door as Jeff entered. Several students stared at him, while Sam's twin cousins, Mandy and Bobby, whispered with their new stepsister, Zoey. For a moment, Sam worried that they might object to Jeff coming into their class. His worry was unfounded. Sweet Zoey waved to Jeff and beckoned him to join them. Although Sam couldn't see Jeff's face, his posture reminded Sam of a scared rabbit about to bolt. He glanced back at the door, so Sam nodded his encouragement and Juliet sent a smile.

Jeff hustled over to the back of the room and dropped into the chair beside Zoey. What a softhearted young lady she was to forgive Jeff for his cruel teasing about her CP and his threats to trip her. Good thing Rob overheard him making plans with his friends and put a stop to it. Rob had also warned Zoey to be careful around those boys, yet her open smile this morning showed only acceptance. Maybe the kindness Zoey and the twins showed him would help him turn his life around. Sam wasn't sure Rob would encourage the friendship, but Zoey's mother, Lauren, was definitely a peacemaker. Maybe her positive input would help.

The teacher, Cameron Northam, one of Sheriff Blake's

new deputies and a marine veteran, welcomed Jeff, then proceeded with the lesson. Sam didn't like to miss Pastor Tim's adult class, but keeping watch on Jeff loomed large.

"I'll stay here," Juliet said. "You go on to your class."

"That's okay." Sam moved away from the door so Jeff couldn't see him hovering like a mother hen. "I want to be sure he doesn't bolt."

"That's not your responsibility."

"I think Judge Mathis would disagree with you." Sam tried to ignore the way her blue eyes reflected the color of her light blue coat, making her all the more beautiful. He didn't dare let down his guard and fall into that trap. "Remember she strongly advised that he should come to church, so I want to be able to personally confirm his attendance."

Juliet sighed. "Right. Okay, so the fellowship hall is over there." She pointed to the open double doors nearby as if Sam hadn't attended this church his whole life. "Coffee?"

"Sure."

In addition to coffee, the welcome ladies served doughnuts and cookies. Sam helped himself to a jelly doughnut and a tall Styrofoam cup of steaming brew. Juliet chose a cream-filled doughnut to accompany her coffee. Sam marked her choice mentally for future reference, though he couldn't imagine why.

"That was really good of you to buy Jeffie a coat." Juliet flashed those gorgeous eyes at him again, but without a hint of flirtation. "I'll pay you back when I get my money from Protective Services."

"Not necessary. Use that money for some clothes and shoes." Sam looked away and nodded to one of the younger welcome ladies, whose stare at him was definitely flirtatious. Sometimes he forgot that being a single Mattson, male or female, came with way too much attention from the opposite gender. "Besides, it wouldn't do for him to get sick." Angry curiosity got the better of him. "Why didn't Dill get him a coat? That's…" Seeing the grief in her eyes, he stopped. "Sorry."

She released a long, weary sigh. "Why didn't Dill do a lot of things differently?" Tears now appeared. "He's my dad, but sometimes it's hard not to hate him."

To avoid the jangle her vulnerability created in his heart, Sam took a sip of coffee and studied the children's artwork on the bulletin board on the opposite wall. His own mom and dad had been the fairest, most decent, most loving parents a kid could have. They'd deserved a better son than he'd been in his teens, but they'd long ago forgiven him for his youthful mistakes. What had it been like for Juliet and Jeff to have a brutal, borderline criminal for a father? To be labeled with a notorious name growing up in a town that wasn't all that forgiving? Although Juliet hadn't grown up in the same house as Jeff, even Petra had been pretty rough around the edges before coming to Jesus.

Juliet nudged him with her elbow. "I think that woman has her eye on you."

Sam didn't have to look to know it was the same woman who'd flirted with him two minutes ago. Besides, looking her way would only encourage her. "That's Erin Farber. She was in our senior class, remember? My mom goes to her beauty shop. Maybe she's looking at your…" Gorgeous blond hair. *Oh, no. You almost put your foot in your mouth.*

Juliet shrugged. "Yeah, I suppose I'm overdue for a trim."

"No, I didn't mean—" Sam took another sip of coffee. "I think I'll get another doughnut. Want one?" *Foot, meet mouth.*

"No, thanks. I think I'll go check on Jeffie."

"Good idea." He dropped his empty coffee cup into the trash and followed Juliet out into the hallway.

The class let out ten minutes later, and most of the students filed out and dispersed, chatting and jostling along the way. Cameron approached Jeff and shook his hand, while the twins and Zoey hung with him.

"Glad to see you here," Cameron said. "I hope you'll come back. And if you have any questions, don't be shy. Just ask away." He nodded to Sam and Juliet. "Hey, folks."

After greetings all around, Cameron excused himself. "See you all in church."

"Miss Juliet," said Bobby, "can Jeff sit with us in church?"

"*May* Jeff sit with us?" Mandy snickered at her twin. He rolled his eyes.

"I don't know…" Juliet glanced up at Sam, another one of their traded looks that were becoming an uncomfortable habit, at least for him.

"Not a good idea." He hated to be the bad cop in this. "The high schoolers sit in the balcony, and—"

"Say no more." Juliet gave the kids an apologetic smile. "Sorry."

Seeing Jeff's scowl and the other kids' disappointment, Sam said, "On the other hand, if you all sit with us and *everybody*—" he gave Jeff a significant look "—behaves well, maybe next week we can let you sit in the balcony."

All four teens grinned, although the innocence in the Mattson trio was offset by Jeff's wily smirk. *Lord, please let Pastor Tim's sermon put a dent in Jeff's rebellious attitude.* After all, this community could extend only just so much grace toward a troubled, troublemaking youth. Unless your name was Mattson. Guilt over his own past pinched at Sam's conscience. Maybe he needed to set an example for the community by extending that grace to a boy named Sizemore.

Juliet gave Jeff a nod to go with the three Mattson kids into a pew with room for four. Sam, Juliet, Mama and Sassy sat behind them. As she slipped into the pew, Juliet glanced across the aisle at Sam's mother, Linda, and gave her a shaky smile. Linda's smile was tight, almost a grimace. She'd seen the lady here at church every Sunday since Mama first persuaded her to attend but hadn't tried to speak to her. She couldn't blame Linda and her husband, Andy, for disliking her. Sam's teen rebellion hadn't been her fault, yet she'd encouraged him to try their patience over the five years she and Sam had dated.

A quiet huff escaped her. What would they say if they learned the precious blonde girl seated between Juliet and Mama was their granddaughter? As far as she could tell, Sam's sister, Sadie, wasn't married and probably didn't have children. With the Mattson tendency toward increasing their clan, surely they hoped Sam and Sadie would add some offspring to the Riverton population, and the sooner, the better. Ah, well. Not her problem.

Sam's hurt and suspicious glances between her and Sassy didn't seem as frequent as before, no doubt because Sassy took after her and Mama. With riding herd on Jeff their only purpose for being together, she prayed Jeff would straighten out soon so Judge Mathis would grant her full custody of her brother and Sam could go back to his own life.

At least Jeff hadn't stormed out of the church when one of the elderly greeters offered condolences to him for the loss of his mother. The man had meant well, of course, but she could see the reminder of her death had stung Jeff. He hadn't spoken of that horrible night when their father murdered Brenda. Didn't seem to want to. She could only pray some hidden anger wouldn't erupt from him in the future, causing him to lash out as Dill often had. Without the money to take him to a therapist, as Judge Mathis had recommended, she could only pray something he heard or learned here in church would help him deal with a situation no child should have to face.

Seated between Bobby and Zoey, Jeff shifted as though uncomfortable, but he did respond when they spoke to him. Listening as best she could with all the chatter going on around them, she could hear them discussing the computer programming team. Last fall, he'd gone with his team to a competition in Albuquerque, and they'd done pretty well for sophomores.

Juliet leaned across Sassy and mouthed to Sam, "Are you hearing this?" At his nod, she grinned. "Now we have another activity he's interested in."

He nodded again.

"I'm interested," Sassy said the same moment the organist began to play.

"Shh." The second Juliet shushed her, she regretted it. Sassy's expression clouded, her lower lip jutted out, and she crossed her arms in a defiant posture. Juliet put her arm around her, but Sassy shrugged her off. Juliet gave her a warning look and hugged her again. And held on tight. After a few seconds, Sassy relaxed, but now her expression had turned sad. Was this how she really felt, or was it an attempt at manipulation? If so, Juliet foresaw having a difficult balancing act between parenting her daughter and saving her brother from following in their father's footsteps.

The worship leader made a few remarks about coming activities, then invited everyone to stand and join in singing with the eight-member praise team. By the second verse of "Lift Up Your Voice to Jesus," Sassy was singing at the top of her lungs *and* in tune.

Was that a grin on Sam's lips as he sang the song's tenor part? Juliet couldn't stop her own smile at her daughter's enthusiasm. Just as quickly, she bit her lips. Letting down her guard like this was way too dangerous. She might need his help with Jeff, but she refused to let these Mattsons accuse her of trying to trap Sam. Yet keeping Sassy's paternity a secret was proving to be a moment by moment challenge.

Before she started coming to church with Mama, Juliet had read only short sentences from the Bible, mostly on greeting cards or memes on Facebook, so every week fed her newfound hunger to learn more. She'd never considered how fascinating the stories might be. Like everybody, she'd heard about Jesus Christ, Adam and Eve, David and Goliath, Noah's ark, even Daniel and the lions' den. But Pastor Tim's preaching from the Old Testament about the kings of Israel and Judah opened her eyes to new stories to think about. Today, he was summing up the way some evil kings passed on their idol worship to their sons who later inherited the throne. And yet some sons of evil kings chose to return to worshipping the God of Israel.

"Having an evil father did not prevent Hezekiah and Josiah from doing what was right in the eyes of the Lord."

As the pastor continued, Juliet noticed a tiny shift in Jeff's shoulders. Did that mean he was listening to the sermon? Did he understand that last point? Or was that wishful thinking on her part? Mama would urge her to pray, so she did. After all, if the Lord could help her escape Dill's influence, He could do the same for Jeff.

Sam thanked the Lord for an answered prayer. The sermon had been better than anything he could have said to Jeff about changing his ways. As usual, Pastor Tim finished his message with his own testimony. At seventeen years old, he'd belonged to a gang because it gave him a sense of family. But their borderline criminal activities left him feeling empty inside, and he'd sensed life should hold more than what he saw around him. The only thing he found to fill that empty place was the Lord Jesus Christ, so he'd trusted Him as his Savior and was welcomed into the Lord's family. The pastor ended with an invitation to anyone who wanted to know more to come forward, either during the final hymn or any day, any time, to talk with him.

Was Jeff listening? Did he know Jesus was calling to him? As Sam joined the congregation in singing the hymn, he prayed for a chance to ask him. The moment the pastor gave the benediction, Jeff turned around.

"So, Sam, where are we going for lunch?" His usual smirk suggested Sam's prayer had not been answered as he'd hoped. Maybe next week…

"We're going home, Jeff." Juliet helped Sassy put on her coat. "Mama has lunch in the slow cooker."

"Yeah, but—"

"But nothing."

"Miss Juliet," Bobby said. "Some of us go for pizza after church. Can Jeff go with us? Our Cousin June will be driving. She's twenty-one and teaches Sunday school."

Sam could see the struggle on Juliet's face. Was it a lack of money that kept her from letting him go? Or something else, like not trusting her brother out of her sight? Should he slip Jeff a twenty so he could pay for his lunch?

Petra beat him to it. "Here you go, Jeff." She chuckled as she gave him a small wad of bills. "I know you'll like pizza better than beans and rice."

"Mama!" Juliet huffed out a breath.

"Thanks, Miss Petra." Jeff pocketed the cash.

The broad smile that lit his face struck Sam in the chest. Even at his worst, his parents never kept him from hanging out with his friends. A trip to the pizza joint with Rob's kids might be just the type of outing to help Jeff turn his life around. Maybe this was the Lord's unique answer to Sam's prayers.

With a crisp winter wind causing them to hug their coats around them, the kids trooped off to join their friends on the church's brown front lawn, which was bordered with patches of dirty snow. After corralling the kids, Sam's Cousin June made sure everybody had a ride with a responsible driver. From the look on Jeff's face, he was as smitten with June as most of the boys. Despite her unassuming ways, at the whole Mattson clan's urging, she'd entered the Miss Riverton Stampede contest coming up in the spring. She'd have a lot of competition with all the talented young cowgirls who lived in the county, but Sam thought she had a pretty good chance of at least making the rodeo queen court.

"Sam, I think Jeff has a crush on your cousin." Miss Petra chuckled in her maternal way.

"Good," Juliet said. "That should put him on his best behavior."

"In theory, at least," Sam added. "Sometimes boys act up when they're trying to get a girl's attention."

Miss Petra laughed out loud, but Juliet scowled at him. "Don't you have someplace to go?"

"Not so fast." Miss Petra nudged her. "With Jeffie gone, we need some help eating our beans and rice. Sam, will you come out to the ranch?"

"Mama!" Juliet shook her head, but Miss Petra ignored her.

Sam's tastebuds had been all set for his mother's usual fantastic casserole at home, but he caught a hint of vulnerability in Miss Petra's expression. This dear lady never seemed to ask for anything for herself yet was always ready to give to others. "Beans and rice sounds great. Can I bring anything?"

"Nope." Miss Petra gave him a broad smile. "Sassy and I will be making cornbread to go with it, won't we, Sassy?"

"Yes, ma'am." The girl beamed at her grandmother.

Not for the first time, Sam studied Sassy's sweet face. She looked so much like Juliet, nobody could doubt who her mother was. But who was her father? Did he really want to know? It was a question he still couldn't answer.

Chapter Eight

"How'd he do?" Sam nodded toward Jeff, who was headed toward the back room to retrieve his coat and backpack.

"Pretty good overall." Rand ran a hand down his jaw. "He's got a gift for organization and an instinct for where to restock the new supplies."

"But?"

Rand's brow furrowed. "He doesn't like to be told what to do because he thinks he knows everything."

Sam chuckled. "Typical teenage boy."

"Maybe."

"Listen, if he crosses any lines, you let me know."

"Will do."

Jeff emerged from the back room. "Can we get a burger on the way home?"

Sam glanced at Rand, who snickered. "Like I said, typical teenager. A bottomless pit."

"Hey." Jeff tried to growl but it came out as a laugh. "I been working hard."

It was already after six, but Sam weighed the idea of driving through Billings' Burgers against calling ahead for pickup at the steakhouse. "Okay. You have to promise to eat Miss Petra's supper. Got it?"

"Got it." Jeff's open smile didn't seem to hold any hidden meanings.

"Now, what do you say to Rand?"

Jeff blinked. "Uh…?" Was he truly this clueless?

"How about thank you?"

"Oh. Oh, yeah." Jeff grinned at Rand. "Thanks."

"See you tomorrow, kid." Rand waved them off before greeting an incoming customer.

Sam drove the three blocks to the burger joint where Juliet was working late today. He hoped Miss Petra had borrowed Raeder's Bronco and picked Sassy up after school. But why was he worried about the little girl? She wasn't his responsibility. On the other hand, this kid was.

After ordering Jeff's burger, fries and milkshake, he drove around to the pickup window, where Juliet awaited them.

"Hey, you two." Her usual guarded expression didn't surprise Sam. "Anything wrong?"

"Just a hungry teenager." Sam handed her his credit card.

"Oh. Okay." She closed the window and returned half a minute later with the card and a receipt. "You don't have to buy him food every day, Sam."

"Hey, don't tell him that," Jeff said. "I'm always hungry after school. And I worked hard today. I deserve it."

"You don't deserve anything. Tomorrow we'll pack a snack." She slammed the window closed.

Jeff's scowl revealed more hurt than defiance. After Juliet brought his order and they drove away, he let the bag sit in his lap and didn't even sip his shake.

"Go ahead and eat." Sam pulled out onto the street. "She's just tired from working all day." Why was he making excuses for her?

Jeff dug into the bag and pulled out the sleeve of fries. "Want one?"

Sam hid a grin. Sharing his food was progress. "Sure. Thanks." Popping the salty fry into his mouth, he felt the grease on his fingers, grease that would stain his new leather steering wheel cover. "Napkin?"

Jeff handed him one, then got busy eating. By the time they reached the Murphy ranch lane, the burger and fries had disappeared, and Jeff was slurping the last of his shake. Time to reveal his surprise.

"So, let's head to the barn. I want to show you something." He drove past the house to the old structure that was years past due for rebuilding.

"Yeah, what?"

"Patience, grasshopper." Without thinking, Sam invoked a character from a favorite old television show.

Jeff snorted out a laugh. "Okay, sensei."

That moment of camaraderie lifted Sam's heart almost more than what lay ahead.

After cleaning and securing the kitchen for tomorrow's early crew, Juliet clocked out at eight-thirty and headed home. Mama's old pickup chugged along the highway, with Juliet praying all the way as usual that she would make it home. Raeder had changed the oil, so at least she wasn't leaving a trail of black smoke.

To her surprise, Sam's truck was parked by the lighted barn. Her stomach growled. She should have eaten before leaving work, but since working at Billings' Burgers, she'd had enough of their food to last a lifetime. She parked beside the Ford and climbed out. Inside the barn, she found Sam, Jeff and Raeder in intense conversation while standing outside a stall around a cute little black-and-white heifer.

"Yeah, you can baby her all you want." Raeder studied the animal with a critical eye. "Make her happy, and she'll love you forever."

"And you promise I don't have to sell her for hamburgers?" Jeff sounded doubtful…and sweetly vulnerable.

"Hey, guys." Juliet approached the group.

Did Sam's broad grin mean he was happy to see her or just pleased with himself? Juliet quashed the thought. He was going a long way to help Jeffie, so she shouldn't accuse him of self-interest.

"Hey, Jules." Jeffie's grin was even broader than Sam's. "Look what Sam brought me. She's for my 4-H project."

"Cool." Not cool, but what choice did she have?

"Yeah," Jeffie said. "She's a two-month-old Holstein heifer and can grow up to be a milk cow just like Chloe and Maude."

"Great." Actually, it *was* great, at least for her brother. "So, are these guys going to teach you how to raise her?"

"Sam and Raeder mostly know about raising beef cattle, but I can do some online research and you can take me to the County Extension office to find out the rest."

"Right." Despite her exhaustion, Juliet felt a little kick of appreciation. "Thanks, guys. Now, if you'll excuse me, I'm beat and hungry."

Walking toward the house, she heard footsteps behind her.

"Wait up, Jules… Juliet." Sam came alongside her. "I wanted to let you know Rand gave me a good report on Jeff's work."

"Good. Now he can pay you back for the cow."

"He doesn't have to pay us back. He's doing us a favor

by taking over her care." He chuckled in that annoyingly appealing way of his. "And she's called a heifer, not a cow."

"How is it a favor? Couldn't you sell her?"

"Sure, but this way, she's a tax write-off."

"Of course." Did the Mattsons do anything that didn't involve their money? No, that wasn't fair. Sam had taken Jeffie on as a *pro bono* project. Still, that didn't mean he had to buy Jeffie hamburgers every day. She grinned to herself. Billings' Burgers were way cheaper than those at Mattsons' Steakhouse.

"Something funny?"

They'd reached the fence to the backyard. Why was he still following her?

"Nope. Just glad to have the day over." No. That was a lie, and she'd promised the Lord she wouldn't lie anymore, even about the little things. "Well, actually, I wondered why you came to Billings' rather than your family's place."

"Time, mostly." He opened the gate for her. "Our restaurant is on the other side of town from the road to your place, and it doesn't have a drive-through."

"Ah." She stared up at him, then wished she hadn't. Why did he have to be so handsome? So generous? So... so appealingly masculine? "Well, thanks again."

She forced her eyes away and walked through the gate toward the house. And felt a little disappointed that he didn't follow her. *Stop it!* Giving place to such feelings would only lead to a broken heart.

"You got a name for her yet?" Sam leaned against the stall wall.

"Working on it." Jeff continued to curry the heifer. His gentle strokes surprised Sam. So far, so good with this project.

"Be careful what you choose. She'll have to live with it for a long time. And so will you."

Jeff grinned, something he'd been doing a lot of since Sam picked him up after work. When he saw the heifer, he'd almost come to tears. Sam had given him space while he sorted out his emotions. And when it had been time for supper, Jeff hadn't wanted to leave the critter. Sam's reminder of his promise to eat Miss Petra's supper on top of his burger and fries finally prompted him to go to the house.

Only problem with that was the dear lady's insistence that Sam stay and eat, too. Which meant he had to sit with Sassy and ponder her parentage. Yet he found it easier than expected to give attention to the sweet little girl. She was smart and, true to her name, a little sassy, but that wasn't any different from the girl her mom had been. As he had with Juliet all those years ago, he felt a natural protectiveness for Sassy, something born and bred into every Mattson man worth his salt and nourished by his work with countless kids in vulnerable situations.

He remembered that fateful day in eighth grade when his buddies were razzing him about being such a "boring nice guy." He'd just begun to feel the constraints of being a Mattson, so that teasing ate at his adolescent soul. When one of the guys had dared him to make some snarky remark to Juliet about her rotten family, to his shame, he'd taken the dare. She always ate alone in the cafeteria, her eyes bright with defiance, almost like she was challenging anybody to come to her table...just as he'd often challenged anybody who tried to speak against the Mattson name. The name, which, ironically, he'd been rebelling against himself, if only in his own mind.

But when she'd looked up at him with those blazing blue

eyes, a hint of vulnerability shining out despite her frown, something shifted inside him. He couldn't go through with the dare. Instead, he decided to befriend her, or at least to try. As they talked, he could see that she got him. Got *to* him. And the next five years, they'd been inseparable. He'd dreamed of the day they could commit the ultimate betrayal of both families and elope.

"How about Raven?"

Jeff's question brought Sam back to the present. "Raven. Uh-huh." He'd always associated that name with spunky black fillies, not docile black-and-white heifers.

"You don't like it." The boy's face clouded.

"Didn't say that. She's your heifer." Sam patted the animal's rump. "If you can live with that name, I can."

That brought a grin. He gently grasped the little heifer's face and stared into her eyes. "Okay, Raven, me and you are gonna make a team. We're gonna win blue ribbons, and one day you're gonna make lots of milk."

The heifer gazed up at Jeff with seeming trust, and Sam felt a kick of satisfaction in his chest. For the first time since he'd been wrangled into this relationship, he felt certain he could make a difference in Jeff Sizemore's life.

On Tuesday evening, Juliet ignored the looks from the other parents as she and Sam herded Sassy and Jeff into the local County Extension Office, part of the county fair and rodeo complex. Her kids had as much right to be here as the others, and if anybody gave them trouble, they'd have to deal with her.

No, that was the old Juliet. But how would Jesus want her to react so she could protect her daughter from the cruel teasing she'd endured as a kid? She knew one thing for sure. She had to maintain a positive attitude, no matter what anyone said to them. Was that thought from the Lord?

"Welcome, y'all." Seated at a table with various paperwork spread out in front of her, the middle-aged registrar, Nancy Snow, gave them each a smile. "We're so glad you're here, Jeff." Her warm expression backed up her words. Nancy, a friend of Mama's, had always been kind.

Jeff's hunched shoulders straightened a little, and he gave her a sober nod.

"And you must be Sassy." Nancy greeted her with the same tone, not speaking down to her as many adults did with younger kids.

"Yes, ma'am." Sassy's broad grin revealed spaces next to her four front teeth where more grownup teeth would soon emerge. "I'm gonna raise chickens."

"Very good." Nancy didn't even glance up at Juliet to see if she agreed to the project. "Let's get your paperwork filled out." She handed Sassy some sheets, then others to Jeff. "What do you plan for your project?"

Jeff cast a nervous glance at Sam. "A hei—" His voice broke, and he reddened as he cleared his throat. "A heifer. A Holstein heifer."

"Awright!" Nancy nodded with enthusiasm. "You get those filled out and bring them back to me." She looked past Juliet's little group. "And who do we have here?"

"Me!" Peanut Westfall, backed by his father, hopped up to the table. "I'm gonna raise chickens with Sassy."

"Well, isn't that something?" Nancy handed him the requisite papers. "You're gonna make a terrific Cloverbud." She gave Raeder a maternal wink, then glanced at his cane. "You doing okay?"

"Yessum. Getting better every day."

While Raeder and Nancy discussed Peanut's registration, Juliet tried not to look over Sassy's shoulder as her daughter carefully printed each line of information. Sam seemed to have the same problem with Jeff until Jeff turned his shoulder to block his view.

"Hmm. Guess I know when I'm not needed." Chuckling, he put his Stetson back on. "See you all tomorrow."

Juliet bit back her disappointment. "Right. Tomorrow." Try though she might, she couldn't keep her eyes off him as he strode from the large meeting hall and out the door. Why did he have to be so good-looking? Such a cowboy? But she had to stop thinking that way. It was what got her into trouble to begin with.

When she turned back to the kids, she saw Jeff across the room with his friend Ethan and, to her shock, one of their distant relatives whose mother was a Sizemore. With none of her cousins close to her age, she'd been on her own in high school and at the mercy of the mean girls. Reminding herself not to return to the past, she shrugged off the memory.

Belle Sizemore Winston waved to her across the room. Juliet waved back, glad to see her here with Oliver. That meant Juliet wasn't the only one who hoped involvement with 4-H would help redeem their family's name. Maybe the boys could encourage each other to better behavior. If only Sam hadn't left before this new development.

Hairdresser Erin Farber sat with a circle of girls discussing sewing patterns. Last Sunday in the church fellowship hall when Erin had flirted with Sam, Juliet hadn't recognized her at first because her hair was now blond instead of its original brown. She'd been Erin Sanderson in high school, and she'd been one of the mean girls. Not the worst, but all too eager to please the pack's leader, Jennifer. Since coming to Jesus, Juliet had tried her best to forgive them all. Surely, like her, they'd all matured beyond their youthful cruelties.

The general 4-H meeting was called to order, and Juliet found seats for herself and Sassy. Two rows in front of them, Lauren Mattson sat with her three teenagers and their little sister, Clementine, who gave Sassy a friendly wave. Jeff sat with his buddies near the back of the room, so she would have to keep watching over her shoulder to be sure he didn't leave.

"That's Ginny Gray from my class," Sassy whispered, pointing to the girl beside Erin.

From the looks of her, Ginny was Erin's daughter. Juliet's heart sank. So the apple hadn't fallen far from that tree. Just one more place where she would have to protect Sassy from cruel teasing. *Lord, please help us. We have so much to do to overcome our family's name.*

But if they kept running into unforgiving people, how would they ever manage to do it?

Chapter Nine

"Ollie's pa's been visiting Dad in prison." Jeff's earlier positive mood had turned dark now that they were in the truck headed home. "I want to visit him, too."

Glancing at wide-eyed Sassy, Juliet swallowed a sharp retort. Her daughter still asked about Dill murdering Jeff's mother, making her fear of her grandfather obvious. Juliet didn't intend to change it.

"We'll have to see about that." Over her dead body.

Bad choice of words! She needed to keep her thinking clear about this. The last thing her brother needed was any influence Dad might have over him. She didn't even trust herself to talk to Dill. In all her twenty-eight and a half years, he'd never given her even one piece of good advice. The worst had been his stopping her from eloping with Sam, which destroyed her life. Then, despite Dill's orders and only by the Lord's good grace, she'd refused to end her pregnancy. She hadn't seen him after Mama helped her move to Colorado, but after she moved to Santa Fe when Sassy was three, he, Brenda and Jeff visited her. To hear him talk, having Sassy as his granddaughter was his proudest accomplishment, something *he* had done. It was his way of taking control, something Juliet would not allow. After that, she refused to let him see Sassy. Yet deep inside, Juliet could still sense a little bit of that young girl who longed for her father's approval. What child didn't feel that way, even when they became an adult?

"So, you two." Time to get this conversation on a positive note. "You're going to be responsible for keeping up your record books Nancy gave you. You need to record everything about your project, from building the chicken coop and currying Raven to the kind of feed and vitamins you give them. Sassy, since you and Peanut are working together on the chickens, you'll need to help him record his activities."

The change of subject worked. Sassy's face brightened, and she launched into a list of tasks she looked forward to, while Jeff stared out into the darkened passing landscape, shoulders hunched in his usual sullen mood. Hadn't his time with his buddies helped at all? Probably not when Dill became the only thing he brought up about their conversation.

"And Mr. Sam says before we get the baby chicks, we need to research the kind of feed that's best for them." She chattered on, saying she wanted to learn about the various nutrients healthy laying hens needed to grow up right.

Sam was so thoughtful to teach Sassy about her project and, of course, Jeff. If only he knew he was pouring all of this effort into his own daughter.

For the first time ever, it occurred to her that he could have married at any time and had other children, ones he could proudly raise in the Mattson tradition. Why hadn't he married? Not that she cared, but she couldn't help being glad because it sure would have complicated matters. What wife would want a man to help his old girlfriend with a kid he didn't even know was his? Juliet chuckled to herself. Thank the good Lord for His mercy. And why hadn't she married? Or even dated? Other than the fact that most guys who seemed interested in her disappeared when they found out she had a child, she'd never found any man who measured up to Sam.

Was she foolish not to tell him Sassy was his daughter? It only took one day to remember why it wasn't at all foolish. Midmorning on Wednesday, Erin Farber showed up at Billings' Burgers.

"So, Juliet." Erin flipped a lock of her long, stylishly tousled, bleached-blond hair over her shoulder. "Looks like you have your hooks into Sam…again. How did you manage that?"

"Didn't manage anything." Hating her own feeling of defensiveness, Juliet kept wiping down tables in preparation for the lunch rush, such as it was most days. "He's Jeff's co-guardian so my brother doesn't have to go into juvie." Might as well recognize the proverbial elephant in the room everybody in Riverton knew about.

"Convenient, I'd say." Erin smirked. "Just don't think you'll ever get the approval of the Mattson clan. They know a gold digger when they see one."

Juliet clenched her jaw. *Lord, help me.* "Say, I really appreciated Pastor Tim's sermon last Sunday. Isn't it remarkable the way the Lord turned his life around from being a gang member when he was a teenager?"

Erin gaped at her and blinked. "Yes. Of course."

"You want to order some lunch?"

"From here? Ugh. No." She moved toward the door. "Say, you should make an appointment with me. I have my own beauty salon, you know. I could restyle your hair into something more flattering." With that final stinger, she left.

While anger tried to worm its way into Juliet's thoughts, she reminded herself to consider the source. Not only was Erin still a mean girl, but she was also teaching her child to be the same. And what was the story behind Ginny having a different last name? Maybe Erin had some deep hurts in her own life and wanted to make other people as unhappy as she was. Juliet paused in her dining room prep. When and how had she begun to think kindly about a person who'd only been *un*kind to her? Only by watching Mama's example and, mostly, with the Lord's help. Just one of the many ways He was changing her.

Even so, Erin had accomplished her mission. Nothing else could have warned Juliet off from telling Sam about Sassy more than the reminder that the Mattsons would never accept her or any other Sizemore into their circle of friends, much less into their wealthy, prominent family. Juliet certainly couldn't expect Sam to forgive her for keeping the truth from him. Learning Sassy was his daughter might even anger him enough that he would stop helping her with Jeff. And until Jeff sorted out his own feelings about Brenda's death and his relationship with Dill, she couldn't risk that.

The weight of her last name and the legacy it brought with it lay heavily on her shoulders. Would she ever be able to escape it? Not only for herself but for Sassy and Jeff? If everybody viewed her like Erin did, that was highly unlikely. If money were no object, she'd pack up her daughter and brother and relocate someplace in Colorado before Dad's trial for Brenda's murder, which would probably stir up more animosity toward her family. Sadly, they were stuck here with no possibility of escaping the coming circus.

Sam's bright idea of getting Jeff an after-school job meant he had to drive him home at quitting time every day. Actually, it was turning out to be a better situation than meeting the school bus because it gave him more time to get important work done in the office. In addition today, with Cousin

Will's wife, Olivia, expecting a baby, he'd agreed to pick up their two dogs from the vet and drive them out to Safe Haven Ranch. He'd have to get them before taking Jeff home.

The pups were about nine or ten months old, but due to Will and Olivia's training, they were pretty well-behaved. DNA testing had revealed their mother was Cousin Rob's registered border collie, Lady. Their father was some unknown mongrel, so they couldn't be registered. Rob had intended Lady for cattle herding, but she'd proven to be a better companion to Rob's new stepdaughter, Zoey, helping with her CP symptoms. The mystery remained over who had stolen Lady, but the pups brought a lot of joy to Will and Olivia's newly blended and growing family.

"Hey, where'd you get the dogs?" Jeff climbed into the truck and reached into the back seat to pet them, receiving slobbery kisses for his attention. Then he inhaled sharply, sat back and stared out the truck's windshield.

After Sam pulled away from the curb and into traffic, he glanced at Jeff. "Something wrong?"

"No." His answer came quick and sharp.

"Okay." Sam grunted. "To answer your question, the dogs belong to Will. I'm taking them back—"

"Where'd he get 'em?"

Sam had decided to go with the flow in dealing with Jeff, so he didn't correct him for interrupting. "They just showed up in a cardboard box down by the river along Will's property."

A sound suspiciously like a sob escaped the boy. "Th-that's awesome." His tone spoke volumes as he reached back and petted the nearest pup. "Hey, fella."

"You want to tell me what's going on?"

They rode in silence for maybe a mile. Then Jeff heaved out a sigh.

"I put 'em there."

"What?" Sam's thoughts had wandered to other matters.

"The pups. I put 'em there last spring. May, I think."

"You did?" Sam came close to exploding in relieved laughter. After all this time, at least part of the mystery was solved. "How'd you happen to have them?"

Another silence. Finally, "My dad stole Rob Mattson's border collie. He was gonna forge registration papers and breed her with another purebred and sell the pups, but our mutt got to her first. When she had these two puppies and they were a couple of weeks old, Dad told me to take them down to the river and drown them." He let out a long, deep sigh. "Man, I'm so glad somebody found them. I hoped they would." Now a full-blown grin lit up his face.

Sam swallowed the emotion rising in his throat. Revealing what Dill did took courage and showed Jeff was maturing well, but it wasn't the whole story. How did he get the pups down to the river? And how did Lady end up near Santa Fe, where Lauren and Zoey found her? First things first.

"Did you carry them all the way out there from town?"

Jeff snorted. "Me walk that far? Ha." He shot Sam a grin. "I've been driving my dad home when he's drunk since I was twelve."

"Hmm." Did Juliet know that? Maybe she'd done the same thing before her parents divorced. "But you didn't do what your dad said with the pups."

"No way." Jeff gave a quick shake of his head, then glanced back at the dogs. "They might be half mutts, but they're cute little critters." He paused and stared out the side window. "Nobody should be drowned just because they're a mistake."

Sam mulled over his comment. These few minutes reinforced what he'd seen in Jeff's preference for a heifer to raise for milking rather than a steer to raise for sale at market. Despite his plans to harm Zoey last fall, there was a tender heart buried deep in his chest.

"Or beat to death because they can't—" Jeff stopped on a sob.

Sam's heartbeat seemed to halt. This was a real breakthrough. *Lord, what should I say now?*

"You've got that right." Pause. "Want to tell me more?"

Shaking his head, Jeff swiped the back of his hand across his eyes. Was he trying to unsee his mother's death? *Lord, please help him because I sure don't know how.* Only one thing came to mind. Juliet should know about this. After delivering the pups to Will, they drove to the Murphy ranch. Her truck was parked outside the farmhouse, so Sam parked and shut off the motor.

"Want to go check on Raven?"

"Sure." Leaving his backpack on the truck floor, Jeff hopped out and jogged toward the barn.

Chuckling at the boy's seeming forgetfulness, Sam carried the backpack to the house. It would provide a good excuse for going in. Not that he needed an excuse. Well, yes, he did. His relationship with Juliet had gotten skittish, like they were both trying to avoid each other but knew they couldn't because of Jeff. Somehow that didn't bother him as much as it had from the beginning. In fact, tonight, he sort of looked forward to seeing her. Not because of Jeff's comments, but…why? This was getting dangerous. He couldn't afford to let her get under his skin only to have her break his heart again.

Seeing Sam approaching the back door with Jeff's backpack, Juliet opened it. "Hey. Come on in." She glanced beyond him. "Where's Jeff?" She laughed. "Let me guess. He's checking on his little heifer."

Sam grinned at her with that gorgeous cowboy smile, and she felt a little hiccup in her chest. Ugh! If only she could stop these involuntary reactions to him. After today's encounter with Erin, she didn't dare let him occupy real estate in her head and especially not in her heart.

"You got that right." Sam handed her the backpack. "Can we talk a minute?"

"Sure."

"Come on in, Sam," Mama called from the kitchen. "Can you stay for supper?"

"Um, well…"

"That's a yes," Mama said as she returned to her meal prep. "Text your mama and tell her I'm feeding you."

Sam chuckled. "Yes, ma'am."

"Let's go into the living room." Juliet set the backpack by the stairs to the second floor.

"Actually, I think Miss Petra should hear this, too." He glanced beyond her. "Is your daughter around?"

Your daughter, too, Juliet's traitorous heart protested. "No, she's out with Raeder and Peanut working on the chicken coop."

"Good. I mean…" Sam shrugged. "She doesn't need to hear this."

"Sure." Juliet tried to still her pulse. "What happened?"

"This is only for your information. Please don't say anything to Jeff about what I'm telling you."

He repeated the conversation he'd had with Jeff on their trip home.

"Oh, my." Miss Petra wiped her eyes. "That poor boy."

"Wow, this is amazing." Her heart bursting, Juliet longed to hug Sam in gratitude, but she settled for touching his arm. "I can't thank you enough for getting him to open up."

Gazing at her with those intense blue-green eyes, he shrugged and grinned softly. "The Lord was the one who made it happen."

"I can believe that." Juliet looked away to avoid his gaze. "It's like you said, Mama. We have to let him grieve at his own pace."

"You know," Mama said, "I've been thinking about him asking to visit Dill. If you two went with him, do you think that would help? I mean, he hasn't seen his dad since..."

"What?" Sam scoffed. "When did he ask to see Dill?"

"The other night after 4-H. His Cousin Ollie's father's been visiting Dad, and Dad told him he wants to see Jeff." Not her, of course, just Jeff, because obviously Dill didn't need anything from her at the moment. "I don't like it."

"Hmm." Sam's brow furrowed. "Miss Petra, what are you thinking?"

Mama stirred the soup, then set down the spoon and faced them. "Maybe seeing Dill in prison will open Jeff's eyes to what his father is and how his own life needs to be different. Maybe he'll see he needs Jesus to make it different."

Juliet traded a look with Sam. His eyes flickered with interest, but whether for Mama's idea or for Juliet, she couldn't tell. Oh, no. Better not go in that direction.

"If you think this will work," he said, "I can try to make it happen. I'll ask Judge Mathis if it's a good idea."

Despite her reservations, Juliet said, "Sounds like a plan." Surely the judge would forbid it.

To her disappointment, that wasn't the case. The next morning, Sam sent her a text saying it was a go. Next Tuesday, Jeff could visit Dill in prison as long as either Sam or Juliet stayed with them the whole time. All day Saturday, Jeff went from being excited about seeing their dad to being nervous about the same. Juliet was glad he had Raven to take care of, homework to do and chores with Raeder to complete. He was on his best behavior as he looked forward to church, or at least to meeting up with his newfound friends.

"Okay, you can sit in the balcony. Right over there." Sam pointed to a spot clearly visible from his own usual pew. "Don't make me come up there."

At his paternal tone, Juliet smothered a laugh and forced a somber expression. "That's right. You don't want the wrath of Sam coming down on you."

"The wrath of Sam?" His Cousin Rob approached with his family. "That's a new one." He waggled a finger at his own teenagers. "Better to be scared of the wrath of Rob. You don't want to lose any privileges, right?"

While his three teens laughed, Jeffie cringed. Was he thinking they might take away his visit to Dad? Despite Juliet's doubts about the visit, she didn't want Jeffie—*Jeff*—she reminded herself, to have any more disappointments in life. Maybe that wasn't realistic, but she couldn't stop that longing. The one positive occurrence today was the friendly greeting to Sassy from Rob's nine-year-old daughter Clementine. After a few moments of further negotiation and promises from the girls to behave, the parents allowed the little girls to sit next to each other.

As always, Pastor Tim's sermon seemed exactly what Juliet needed. Today he spoke about trusting the Lord through the storms of life. "Yea, though I walk through the valley of the shadow of death, I will fear no evil: for Thou art with me," he quoted from Psalm 23. Trusting that promise was meant for her as well as all other believers in Jesus, Juliet believed in her heart He would be with her and Jeff during Tuesday's unwanted visit to their father.

Try as she might though, she couldn't maintain that feeling as Sam drove her and Jeff to the Penitentiary of New Mexico some fourteen miles south of Santa Fe. True to her mood, the steel gray skies overhead appeared heavy with snow, and the wind blew across the highway as though trying to stop their progress. Once inside the stark, pinkish-gray building, they endured a thorough security inspection and left all personal belongings in the care of the officers. Then two guards led the three of them into a large room with high, barred windows, furnished with tables and chairs, where prisoners could meet with visitors under the supervision of more guards.

"There's my boy!" Despite his manacled hands, Dill strutted in like he was in a parade. The guard at his elbow whispered a warning of some sort, and Dill smirked at him. "Yeah, yeah, I know. I'll be good." He didn't even spare a glance at Juliet, but she hadn't expected anything from him.

Beside her, Jeff sniffed back tears and cleared his throat. They both knew Dad's abhorrence of any kind of crying. Jeff took a step toward him, but Sam gripped his shoulder.

"Sorry, Jeff. Remember. No touching."

"Whatever." Jeff shrugged him off. "Hey, Dad." The uncertainty in his voice brought up Juliet's own tears. Despite his progress these past few days, her dear brother was setting himself up for heartbreak.

Chapter Ten

"Well, son, how's school?" Dill Sizemore focused all his attention on his son, not even glancing at Juliet.

Sam barely knew the man, but he seemed determined to create a divide between his two children as he chatted only with Jeff. He clearly wanted to charm the boy, who ate up his attention with near desperation. When Jeff told Dill about Raven, Dill sneered briefly but appeared to catch himself.

"Yeah, I know what you mean. One year, when that was my ranch, I hand-raised me a prime Texas Longhorn steer. Sold him for three thousand dollars."

Beside Sam, Juliet shifted in her chair. Dill had never owned the Murphy ranch, but here he was boasting as though he had. The man clearly did not know his son if he thought selling a steer he'd raised would impress Jeff.

But Jeff surprised him. "That's cool, Dad. Next time I'll do that."

"So, did you go out for basketball like I told you to? That was my best sport, so you're probably real good at it."

"No, sir." Jeff gave Dill a sheepish grin. "Remember? I'm more into computers."

Dill snorted with obvious disgust. "Ya gotta use your body, boy. Build up those muscles so you can be strong."

He cast a disparaging look at Sam, as though he were some sort of threat. "You never know when you'll need it." He glanced at the guard hovering nearby, then hunched over the table toward Jeff in a secretive posture. "Listen, I want you to know I forgive you for not remembering that night like it really happened."

"What?" Jeff's troubled frown spoke volumes.

"Yeah, boy. You didn't think I saw you, but I know you had a few drinks."

"But—"

Dill interrupted him and glared at Sam. "I told him never to drink, but what can you do?" He snickered. "I seem to recall you liked to sneak drinks from your pa's stash when you were this age."

Sam's father never touched a drink in his life, much less owned a liquor supply. "This isn't about me, Dill. Just talk to your kids." If he couldn't bait him to acknowledge Juliet, at least he'd tried.

"Aw, now. Is that any way to talk? I know a few of your secrets, don't I?"

Beside Sam, Juliet sucked in a soft breath, but he forbade himself to rise to this strange question. The man knew nothing about him that wasn't common knowledge all over Riverton. What a manipulator.

"But, Dad—" Jeff's voice took on a pleading tone.

"No, no." Dill waved his manacled hands in a dismissive gesture. "I forgive you for telling the cops I hurt your mother. I know you just wanted to hide your drinking so we wouldn't get in trouble for it. I can appreciate that. But when she fell and hit her head, I wasn't anywhere close to her. You were. You tripped her. Remember?"

Jeff's face was a study in confusion, almost as if he was

trying to picture that horrible night in a way different from what he'd told the cops.

"You know, boy, it's a criminal offense to lie under oath. Not only can you be sentenced to jail, but your mama's folks and mine won't look kindly on it. You don't want to live with regrets like that, do you?"

Jeff gulped. "No, sir." His eyes misted.

"Aw, now, boy, don't you be crying. No son of mine cries like a sissy. Just be thinking back on that night so you can remember what really happened in a way that gets your daddy out of jail for something he didn't do."

"You despicable lying beast." Juliet jumped to her feet. "Come on, Jeff. I think we've seen all we need to of this murdering monster."

"Ma'am." The guard stepped closer to her, with another one right behind him. "Calm down, or you'll have to leave."

"Don't worry. I can't get out of here fast enough. Come on, Jeff."

"Dad?" The plaintive note in Jeff's voice touched Sam's core.

"Go on, boy." Dill lounged back in his chair like he was a potentate dismissing a minion. "You know what to do."

Sam followed the siblings from the room feeling like he needed a shower. Or to throw up. Dill Sizemore was the proverbial piece of work. Would Sam and Juliet ever be able to undo the damage that evil man had done to Jeff by somehow suggesting the boy had caused his mother's death? And he'd basically snubbed Juliet instead of thanking her for taking care of Jeff. But as angry as it made Sam, it wasn't his place to add fuel to the fire by venting to them.

Yet he was still stewing over the situation on Wednesday morning, so he blew off steam to his law partner and best friend, Cousin Will.

"I've seen some manipulators in my life, but I've never seen anybody try to destroy his own son like that through innuendo and outright lies." Sam plopped his briefcase down on his desk and hung his Stetson on the hat rack. "How could he do that?"

"Well, you know it runs in the family." Will leaned against the doorjamb, arms crossed. "Dill Sizemore isn't the first man in that family to murder his wife in front of their child. At least he didn't have a shootout with the cops. Jemmy still has nightmares from Ed's final confrontation with the law."

"Oh, man." Sam plopped down in his desk chair. "Megan. Bro, I'm so sorry for bringing up bad memories."

Will's only sister had married Ed Sizemore. Like Dill, the man was cruel and violent and had shot Megan in front of four-year-old Jemmy. Will had fought another Sizemore relative for the right to adopt Jemmy and won. Once Will and Olivia married, they changed Jemmy's last name to Mattson so he wouldn't have to carry the infamous name of his father. Anybody who got involved with that family always suffered for it. Just one more reason Sam knew better than to revive his teenage relationship with Juliet. But he was finding it harder and harder to keep his distance when every instinct told him to protect her, especially after their disastrous meeting with Dill at the prison.

"No problem. It's hardly something I can forget." Will gave him a rueful look. "I'll always miss Megan, but for the most part, Jemmy's doing great, thanks to Olivia and Emily." He chuckled. "Emily turned seven last week, but she's already a little mama to Jemmy. They're both excited about the baby."

Admiring his cousin's newly blended family, Sam felt a twinge of envy, which he quickly dismissed. Nobody deserved happiness more than Will, who'd had many struggles growing up. Now he worked hard to make life easier for countless shattered families. Sam tried to emulate him every day. If the Lord ever granted him a family of his own, he'd look to Will for his example of how to treat them.

Every thought of having his own family brought Juliet's face to mind. Ten years ago, they'd planned to elope, yet she'd gotten pregnant by some other man. Even if he forgave her for that betrayal, could he ever trust her again? Despite his misgivings, his heart had begun to tug him in her direction, especially after the way Dill treated her yesterday. Sam's parents had always been loving and supporting, even throughout his years of teen rebellion. His dad was a model of uprightness, generosity and moral support, everything Dill was not. But Sam must not let himself become entangled with Juliet again.

Before Sam picked Jeff up from work that afternoon, he prayed for wisdom in dealing with the boy in the aftermath of their prison visit. Due to the raw emotions in both siblings, he hadn't tried to talk to them about it as he drove them home. After more than twenty-four hours, had they recovered from Dill's outrageous treatment? Despite his prayers, Sam braced himself for some sort of drama.

But Jeff emerged from the hardware store whistling and hopped into Sam's pickup like he was going to a picnic.

"How was your day?"

This was new. When had Jeff ever cared about Sam's day? "Good. And yours?"

"Good." He pulled a sheet of notebook paper from his backpack. "I got a list here of what I need to feed Raven, and Rand says he'll give me a deal on the vitamins if I work every other Saturday."

"Sounds good." Sam checked traffic, then pulled away from the curb. Was Jeff in denial about his father? Or was Sam overestimating his own importance as a counselor to the boy? They'd had a breakthrough last week, but maybe the visit to the prison set Jeff back, and he could only deal with it by pretending his mother's death never happened.

Juliet was another story. As usual, when they arrived at the ranch, Jeff headed for the barn, and Sam carried the backpack inside the house. She greeted him at the back door with dark circles under her eyes…and no smile.

"Hey, you okay?" He hated seeing this spunky woman depressed. Uh-oh. That was dangerously close to caring too much for her again.

"Sure. I'm fine."

"You are not," Miss Petra called from the kitchen. "Tell him you were up all night crying."

"Mama!" Juliet rolled her eyes. "Don't pay her any mind."

Sam carried the backpack to the base of the staircase, then made himself at home at the kitchen table. "Jeff didn't seem to have the same problem in spite of what Dill said. Did he talk it out to either of you?"

"Nope." Miss Petra shook her head. "He still doesn't say much to me." She shrugged. "It's okay though. He's got a lot to sort out." The peace in the lady's eyes gave credence to her words.

"How about you, Jules… Juliet?" He really must stop reverting to his teenage nickname for her during those few sweet years when they'd always known each other's thoughts. "Have *you* sorted everything out?"

She gave him a little grin, almost like she understood

his slip. Almost like she was also remembering the understanding they'd had all those years ago. His pulse skipped a beat before good sense took over. Maybe that understanding had only been wishful thinking on his part.

"Pretty much." She sighed. "I didn't expect anything better than the way he's always treated me. Except when he wants something. Then he can be pretty charming."

"Don't I know it." Miss Petra gave her a sad smile. "But the Lord can make beauty from ashes, honey. Just look at you. I'm so proud of the beautiful, responsible woman you've become." She winked at Sam. "Don't you agree, Sam?"

His collar suddenly felt tight. He should have taken his tie off after work. "Sure. She's doing a great job with Jeff."

"And Sassy," Miss Petra said. "Don't forget Sassy."

"Mama!" Her voice a growl, Juliet glared at Miss Petra. "Stop it."

Something passed between the mother and daughter Sam couldn't grasp. He'd never claimed to understand women's relationships, so he wouldn't try now. Besides, their disagreement wasn't any of his business. Maybe he should leave so they could sort it out.

Seeing Mama's little smirk, Juliet sent her a warning look, then softened her expression. Mama might tease, but she would never betray Juliet. Yesterday when Dad had hinted about knowing some of Sam's secrets, her heart had almost stopped in terror. It was *her* secret, not Sam's, that he knew about. But then, why was he holding on to the truth about Sassy? Did he plan to blackmail Juliet? That would totally be like him. Last evening, she'd unloaded all of it on Mama, and once again, Mama insisted she must tell Sam he was Sassy's father. But until this situation with Jeff was sorted out, Juliet didn't have the emotional strength to deal with the most important issue in her life.

"Will you stay for supper?" Mama asked Sam.

Please say no. Juliet frowned at him, hoping he'd take the hint.

"Miss Petra, how can I resist your ham and beans?" He glanced at the stove, then winked at Mama. "Your cornbread's almost as good as my mom's."

Mama laughed. "Linda's a very fine cook, and you're a good son to recognize it."

"I seem to recall the two of you usually tie for first place in the county fair peach cobbler contest." Sam looked all too comfortable as he chatted with Mama.

Juliet was far from comfortable, especially when Sassy chose that moment to waltz into the kitchen with Peanut in tow.

"Can we have a cookie?" Sassy looked to Mama.

"Me, too?" Peanut said.

"Hey." Juliet put her fists at her waist. "It's me you should be asking, not your gramma. Besides, you know the rules. No cookies before supper." She ignored Sam's chuckle. "Now go wash up, both of you."

"Come on, Peanut." Huffing out a sigh, Sassy grasped the little boy's hand. "Sometimes grownups can be so mean." While she shook her head in disgust, her words held a maternal tone.

Once they left the room, Mama and Sam laughed out loud.

"Sassy sure does live up to her name," Sam said.

Juliet scowled at him. "Why don't you make yourself useful and go tell Raeder and Jeff supper's almost ready."

"Yes, ma'am." He held up his hands in a gesture of surrender, then stood and hustled out the back door.

"Oh, Juliet." Mama gave her a chiding look that was becoming all too familiar. "He's such a good man. I believe with all my heart you can trust him. Why don't you tell him the truth and get it over with?"

"What truth?" Hands still damp from washing, Sassy bounced into the room with Peanut following right behind her.

Juliet's eyes burned, and her throat clogged up. Why couldn't she just do what Mama said?

Mama gave her a sympathetic smile before tapping Sassy's nose. "The truth is that you need to set the table or we'll never get to eat. And Peanut, you can help."

"Humph." Sassy crossed her arms and frowned. "I know that's not what you were talking about, but I'll let you off this time."

Mama chuckled, but Juliet turned away so her daughter couldn't see the emotions at war on her face. As she closed her eyes to blink away the tears, Erin Farber's words flashed through her mind. Sure, she could tell Sam about Sassy, but what good would it do? Even if the Mattsons acknowledged Sassy's paternity, they would never accept her and certainly wouldn't accept Juliet. She had to hold back the truth as long as possible until she could figure a way to protect her daughter from the shame of being—and yet not being—a member of the county's wealthiest family.

Stinging wind whipped around Sam as he strode across the frozen barnyard toward the lighted barn. Come spring, the building sure could use some repairs and a fresh coat of paint. Same for the house. Of course such tasks weren't his responsibility, but living on a well-kept ranch himself, he couldn't help but notice and be pleased to see Raeder had reinforced the weakest parts of the barn's structure so it wouldn't fall down in the coming spring winds.

He waved to the cowhand, who was leading a couple of horses into the side door. "Supper's ready," he called out.

Raeder returned a friendly wave. "Thanks. Be right in."

As Sam entered the main door, he considered the blessing Raeder was to Miss Petra, and she to him. When he'd suffered that near-fatal fall in last year's rodeo, the older lady had insisted that he recover at her place once he was out of the hospital. She said twenty-five was way too young for the widowed father of a little boy to be laid up without any help. And as Raeder recovered, he returned the favor with all the work he did around this place, making the little ranch a warm, welcoming home for its stitched-together family. Oddly, Sam had begun to feel a part of that family. Or maybe not so odd.

He chuckled at the way Juliet had ordered him to fetch Jeff and Raeder. For the most part, she was becoming as welcoming as her mother. It was all for Jeff's sake, of course. Yet Sam didn't feel as though she was using him. She never had used him, except...

As he neared Raven's stall, soft, tearful words reached his ears. Against all he believed in, he crept close to eavesdrop.

"I didn't do it, Raven. I'd never hurt my mom. I mean, I wasn't always nice to her, but I loved her. I can't remember if I had a beer, but I don't think so. Seeing my dad drunk all the time made me see how stupid it was." A sob followed. "I don't care what Ollie or his dad says. I don't have to lie for my dad. I don't want to be like him. I want to be a good man, like Sam."

Feeling like he'd been body-slammed, in a good way, Sam rocked back on his heels, then quietly backed up toward the door. With the wind blowing, he doubted Jeff could hear him.

The kid wanted to be like him? Sam gulped down a riot of emotions. All this time, he'd doubted himself at every turn. *Thank You, Lord. I can't replace his dad, but somehow I've been doing all right. Just help me keep doing the good stuff and not mess this up.*

He slammed the barn door. "Yo, Jeff. Dinner's ready." He couldn't quite keep the emotion from his voice, but again, the wind saved him.

"C-coming." Jeff's head popped up over the side of the stall. "She's done eating."

Sam approached them. "You clean out the stall?"

"Duh!" He swiped a hand down his cheek. "First thing I always do, just like you told me."

Sam managed a chuckle. "Good. And put her blanket on her?"

Now he grinned. "You gotta ask?" He waved a hand toward the orange-and-brown blanket on the little heifer.

"Good job. Let's go eat."

Jeff grabbed his coat from the hook outside the stall. Nothing more had been said about Sam buying it for him, but satisfaction filled him at seeing the boy in something warmer than his jean jacket. Especially as they trudged against the wind to the house. Once Jeff had Miss Petra's beans, ham and cornbread in his belly, he'd be warm in all the right places. Except maybe that empty spot in his heart where a father's love should be. Sam couldn't do anything about that. What had Miss Petra said? Jeff needed to learn that God is a good, good Father.

Not for the first time in the past ten years, Sam thanked the Lord for his own good parents. If not for their forgiveness and love, he would still be adrift in life. Because they'd stuck by him after Juliet crushed his heart, he'd been able to make something of himself, someone even a troubled Sizemore kid could look up to.

Chapter Eleven

"Not so much water, honey." Mama stood in the kitchen doorway monitoring Sassy as she watered the tomato seedlings growing in little pots on the dining room table. "Just a couple of tablespoons for each one. And pour it on the base of the plants, not the leaves."

"Yes, ma'am." Sassy gripped the handle of the large watering can with both hands and gently dripped the liquid into the pots.

"As soon as this March wind dies down, we'll get them in the ground." Mama waved a hand toward the sunny south side of the house where her garden plot lay.

"Let's hope she inherited your green thumb." Juliet studied the variety of vegetable and flower seedlings spread over the table, buffet and two card tables under the bay window. "I've managed to kill everything I've ever tried to grow." Even as a teen, she hadn't helped Mama with her gardening, mostly because she preferred to hang out with Sam instead of staying home and learning how to grow the food they needed to survive. Now that she was a mother herself, she regretted not helping Mama all those years ago.

"Well, now you're back home, so I can teach you how to have a flourishing garden." Mama stepped over to inspect a plant labeled "pumpkin" and pinched off a withered leaf. "If our peach and apple trees have a good harvest, we'll learn all about canning, too. Won't we, Sassy?"

Sassy grinned. "Yes, ma'am. And I wanna make peach cobbler like you do."

"Me, too." Juliet ran a hand down her daughter's long blond hair. "Okay, let's grab a bite to eat before Sam gets here."

Sassy's smile broadened. "I can't wait to see my baby chicks."

I can't wait to see Sam. Juliet had been trying to dismiss such thoughts for weeks, but every time she thought she'd gotten control of her feelings, something happened to sabotage her. Like today. He was using his Saturday to help her bring Sassy's baby chicks from the garden and hardware store. Before that, he, Jeff and Raeder had laid out the chicken yard and built the coop from the kit he'd ordered, including electrical wiring and heat lamps. He never mentioned money. As he'd done with Jeff's winter coat, he saw a need and filled it.

Despite being busy with his job at the law office, he took the kids and her to 4-H meetings and helped the kids keep up their record books. How could she not admire him for his kindness? How could she not look forward to his Saturday visits to Mama's ranch, when he always brought some little gift, like one of his Stetsons he'd outgrown for Jeff to wear? Or a sack of potatoes and a five-pound roast for Mama, claiming he couldn't eat up all her fine cooking without giving something back? The gift that touched Juliet's heart the most was his helping Sassy choose her baby chicks from the catalog and showing her how to order them.

Juliet was sweeping out the mudroom when he arrived

shortly after one. He lifted a large white plastic tub from his pickup and hustled toward the house, fighting to keep the tub from blowing away on this cold, blustery March day. Juliet hurried to open the door.

"What's this?"

"What's this?" echoed Sassy behind her.

"Hi to you, too." Sam shivered as he closed the door. "My internal thermometer says it's time for spring." He set down the tub. "This is for a brooder for the chicks. With more cold weather forecasted for the spring, Rand suggests we keep the chicks in the house until they're about six weeks old. The ones we're getting are just a week old."

"Thanks, Sam." Once again he'd seen a need and taken care of it.

"Thanks, Sam." Sassy echoed her again.

He gazed at Sassy and frowned, in fact, almost winced for a brief moment, then seemed to force a smile. "Okay, ladies, here's what we're going to do."

With Mama's approval, they made space for the brooder among the seedlings in the dining room. He brought in a bag of crushed corncobs for bedding and some pieces of wool to tape to the sides.

"The chicks will huddle together for warmth, and the wool will help them." He surveyed his work and gave a quick nod of satisfaction. "Now, let's go get those chickens."

"Is Peanut coming?" Sassy always wanted to include her sidekick.

Sam shook his head. "Raeder says he's taking a nap. But he should be up and ready to help us when we get back from town."

The wind seemed determined to push Sam's heavy pickup sideways, but he managed to keep it on the highway to town. At Mattsons' Garden and Hardware Store, the three of them hurried inside.

"Hey, guys." Jeff looked up from stacking cans of motor oil in a display. He grinned at Sassy. "What're y'all doing in town?"

"Jeffeee." Sassy rolled her eyes. "We came for my baby chicks."

"Hmm. Baby chicks? I don't think we sell baby chicks."

"Jeffeee!" Sassy stamped her foot. "You do too!"

Juliet grinned at Sam. He chuckled, and she shook her head. Her brother and daughter were more like siblings than uncle and niece. And that was a good thing. Anybody looking in from the outside might think they were a family, with Sam being the doting father.

Oh, no! She must stop that kind of thinking. But once again, her feelings were determined to betray her good sense.

The unmistakable sound of cheeping baby chicks came closer as Rand Mattson wheeled in a cart holding a vented cardboard box.

"Somebody out here order thirty baby chicks?"

"Me! Me!" Sassy bounced around like four-year-old Peanut would, clapping her hands and squealing with delight.

Rand lifted the cover to reveal a brood of tiny yellow, black and red chicks milling around and pecking for grain on the corncob-covered box floor.

Sassy gasped. "Oh, Mommy, they're so cute!" Tears shone in her eyes as she gently petted one after another of the tiny birds. "I promise to take care of them forever."

"I know you will, sweetheart." Juliet blinked back her own tears. She mouthed "thank you" to Sam, and he returned a sweet shrug. From the sheen in his eyes, he was clearly moved by Sassy's delight. Oh, if only he knew. If only she could tell him. Instead, she said, "Sassy, what do you say to Mr. Sam?"

Sassy gave him her sweetest smile. "Thank you, Mr. Sam. I love them."

He cleared his throat. "You're welcome, Sassy. Just remember, when they start laying eggs, I get the first dozen."

There he went again, giving Sassy *and* her the dignity of accepting his help without it being charity. How could she not...*admire* this good man?

Sassy was so adorable in her delight over the chicks. Sam had to swallow the strong emotion trying to rise up in his throat. This must be what it felt like for a man to give his own child a special gift and watch her excitement and happiness. Would he ever experience that feeling? Would he ever have his own family? Oddly, he couldn't see it happening with anyone but Juliet. But he also couldn't see it happening with her. Once bitten, twice shy. He'd never be able to fully trust her. Besides, someday Sassy's birth father might come along and claim her or, at the least, cause trouble for Juliet. Either way, Sam had no idea how he'd react. Best not to let his emotions run away with him.

In the meantime, as long as Judge Mathis required him to keep Jeff in line, he had to put one foot in front of the other and keep going. That meant doing for Sassy whatever he did for her uncle so the precious little girl didn't feel left out. Taking the kids to 4-H had turned out to be more fun than he expected. It was a great program he should have been more involved in as a kid instead of half-heartedly working on his projects.

Making sure Juliet took the kids to church also reaped some benefits. Sassy loved Sunday school and always repeated her lesson to Sam and Juliet before the main service began. One Sunday in late March, she announced that she loved Jesus and had invited Him into her heart. Sam once again felt a paternal joy for the little girl. For Jeff, not so much. The teen was doing well at work, improving in school, and even behaved himself in the church balcony with Rob and Lauren's kids. But talk about the Lord had him yawning or sighing with obvious boredom. With Easter just around the corner, Sam prayed the boy would finally understand what the resurrection of Jesus Christ was all about.

On Palm Sunday, Sam's parents shocked him by inviting Juliet to sit with them. "It's time we put the past where it belongs," Mom said to him. To Juliet, she said, "I called Petra, and she said it's okay to invite you and your kids to dinner at our house after church."

"I… I…" Juliet blinked in surprise. In fact, Sam thought he saw a flicker of fear in her eyes. But she cleared her throat and offered a shaky smile. "Thank you. That's very kind of you. But I need to drive Raeder and Peanut home—"

"Don't mind us, Miss Juliet." Raeder joined them, with Peanut at his side. "I'm doing a lot better, so I can drive Miss Petra and us back to the ranch."

"And Sam will drive you home later," Dad said. "Right, Sam?"

Were they all ganging up on him? He couldn't stop this foolishness without causing a scene. "Yeah, sure." He gave Juliet a smile that felt more like a grimace.

She offered back a rueful smile. Obviously she didn't want this any more than he did.

After church, Sam drove Juliet and the kids out to the Double Bar M Ranch. Juliet and Jeff had been there in February, but for Sassy, it was a brand-new adventure. Before they followed Mom and Dad inside their house, she ran to the fence of the north pasture, where the large herd of Angus steers grazed and young calves scampered around.

"That's a lot of cows," she said, her blue eyes wide with wonder. "Whatcha gonna do with all of 'em?"

"They're gonna be your next hamburger." Jeff tweaked Sassy's nose.

"They are?" She brushed Jeff's hand away and turned to Sam, curiosity beaming from those bright eyes.

Sam chuckled. "Yep. That's how your hamburgers start out. But first they have to go up to summer pasture in the Sangre de Cristo Mountains."

Now Jeff perked up. "You mean you go on a trail drive?"

"No, not me." Sam considered how to make the most of this interest. "I'm not involved in that part of the ranch, except sometimes I help with branding. And it's not an actual trail drive. The cowhands truck the herd up into the mountains."

"Wow." Sassy gave Sam an admiring smile. "Are you a real cowboy, Mr. Sam?"

His heart stirred at the wonder in her face. "Sort of…"

"I want to go with the herd," Jeff said. "That'd be so cool."

Sam mulled the idea. "Maybe. But you should talk to Bobby." He waved at Rob and his family as they unloaded from their ride outside the Big House. "He went on the drive to bring them down last fall and can give you the lowdown on rounding up the herd. First you have to learn to ride."

"I can ride." Jeff's face lit up again. "Raeder's been teaching me."

"Okay, but riding herd on a lively cowpony is a lot different from trotting around the corral on an old rescue horse."

"Yeah, but—"

"And with that—" Juliet took Sassy's hand and headed toward the house "—let's not keep Mr. and Mrs. Mattson waiting."

From her hunched shoulders as she walked, Sam could tell she was still nervous. He was dealing with his own nerves. What did Mom expect to gain from having Juliet and the kids come out to the ranch? And why hadn't she mentioned her plans to him before church? Easy answer. She didn't want him to stop her. Was she trying to be a matchmaker between Sam and a Sizemore? What had changed her mind about that notorious family from just a few weeks ago, when neither of his parents could say a good word about a single one of them? And how was he going to stop her foolish plotting? Because no way was he going to rekindle his teenage romance with Juliet. Help her? Yes. But let himself love her again? No way.

Juliet had never been in Sam's parents' house. It was one of three domiciles on the ranch. The original Big House was an elegant two-story antebellum mansion that sat on a hill overlooking the Rio Grande. Rob and his family lived there. Sam had told her the attractive pink one-story adobe hacienda sitting a few hundred feet away was a guest house. He lived with his folks, Andy and Linda, whose traditional two-story Queen Anne farmhouse was nearer the front entrance of the property. If not sitting in the shadow of the larger Big House, this house, with its wraparound porch and railings and gabled roof, would be impressive in many settings.

Inside, the cozy decor suggested a welcoming atmosphere, but Juliet felt anything but welcome. Why had Linda invited her and the kids out here? Did she and Andy suspect the truth about Sassy? When Juliet was in her teens—and still today—her reputation had been linked to her family's name, so everyone seemed to think her morals weren't exactly exemplary. To be fair to them, before meeting Jesus, she'd often lied. But she'd had one absolute truth. Sam was the only boy in her life, the only one she'd ever been intimate with. While the memory brought shame now that Juliet was a Christian, Mama often reminded her God never made a mistake. He could bring something good even from our worst behavior. And nothing in her life was more wonderful than Sassy.

Juliet joined Linda in the kitchen to help her lay out dinner, which centered around a large baking dish filled with delicious smelling chicken enchilada, with salad, salsa and chips on the side. Juliet laughed softly, then bit her lip. It wouldn't do to offend her hostess.

"Something funny?" Linda's warm tone helped ease Juliet's concern.

"Sorry. No." She laughed out loud. "Just that I expected y'all to eat beef in some form at every meal."

Linda laughed too. "That's what I thought when I married Andy. He said steaks and roasts could get pretty old and gave me leave to come up with as many other meats as I wanted to serve."

"Smart man."

"Yes, he is." Linda's expression grew thoughtful. "I'm so blessed. Our thirtieth anniversary is coming up this summer, and I've never had a moment of regret for marrying him."

Her words struck Juliet's heart. What would such an enduring love to a good man be like? But the only good man she would ever consider was out of her league and only spending time with her because Judge Mathis required it for Jeff's sake. Her teenage romance with Sam would never be rekindled.

Once everyone was seated, the conversation around the table centered on Pastor Tim's sermon. Andy Mattson taught the adult men's Sunday school class, and it was clear he knew the Bible well.

"Jeff, before you take another bite of Miss Linda's fine cooking, answer me this. What did you learn today about the significance of Palm Sunday?" His dark blue eyes focused on Jeff, who squirmed in his seat next to Sam. Juliet's heart went out to her brother. If she felt uncomfortable in this house, how much more must he feel being here?

"Man." Jeff let out a breath, then laughed nervously. "I didn't know there'd be a quiz. Shoulda listened better."

While Andy and Sam chuckled, Juliet released a quiet sigh. Why was Jeff so opposed to anything to do with church?

"I know." Sassy raised her hand.

Andy gave her a kindly smile, and Juliet's heart dipped. He'd make a wonderful grandfather to Sassy, if only…

"Awright, little miss. You tell us." His cowboy drawl added to his warmth.

Sassy grinned and sat tall in her chair. "Jesus was showing everybody that He was the King of kings. The people thought He would make the mean Romans leave their country, but He was a different kind of King." Her face grew serious. "He was gonna die for our sins that very week."

"That's right." Andy winked at her. "I see you know your Bible stories."

"Yessir." She gave him another big grin and dug into her enchilada.

Seated across from Sam, Juliet noticed his intense gaze on Sassy as she spoke. What was he thinking? Could he see a hint of Mattson in their daughter? Probably not. Still, she couldn't wait for this meal to end so she could get them back to the safety of Mama's ranch, where nobody could ferret out her secrets and threaten to destroy her and Sassy's and Jeff's lives. Until then, she must keep smiling and try to show these folks she'd changed from the less-than-honest girl she'd always been until she'd met Jesus.

Only, if she were all that honest, if she'd truly abandoned all her lying ways, wouldn't she tell these people right here and right now that Sassy was their granddaughter?

Keeping her smile in place, she gave herself a mental shake. No doubt if she made such an announcement, they'd kick her out of this fancy house as a gold digger. And until she could trust that Sam would continue to help her with Jeff, she didn't dare risk it.

Chapter Twelve

In mid-May, the Riverton Fair and Rodeo opened for a week of celebration, with most businesses shutting down or working only half days. The fair's first afternoon and evening included midway rides and food trucks, with the Miss Riverton Stampede skills competition taking place in the rodeo arena.

Sam had always been proud of his younger cousin June, and he was even prouder to watch her show off her roping and barrel racing skills as she competed for the title. Although the Mattson name carried a lot of weight locally and statewide, the rodeo committee always brought in judges from other states who could judge the five finalists impartially. But to Sam and his relatives, nobody could beat this talented young lady. Beside and behind him in the bleachers sat a posse of Mattson parents, cousins, aunts, uncles and various friends and shirttail relations who came to show their support for their favorite cowgirl.

"That's Miss June!" Little Peanut jumped up in his seat in the bleachers. "She's my Sunday school teacher. Yay, Miss June!"

"That sure is Miss June." A hint of interest lit Raeder's eyes as he grabbed Peanut's waist to keep him from falling into the aisle.

A few seats away, Sam watched the cowboy as he cheered along with everyone else. What was the story there? He couldn't think of a better match for June, especially when she rode past them and glanced Raeder's way and Sam noticed a hint of interest in her eyes as well. If she was chosen Miss Riverton Stampede or one of the runners-up, she'd serve for a year but only if she remained single. Whoa. Why was he thinking about marriage? Maybe because Mom kept sending pointed hints his way.

That evening, gathered in the grand exhibition hall of the Riverton Cattlemen's Association, the crowd watched as the contestants showed off their softer side in pretty Western-style evening gowns, complete with fancy jeweled boots and matching cowgirl hats. The next event—their speeches stating why they were interested in the title—revealed their dedication to the Stampede and the Western way of life. Finally, the Big Boss of the Stampede, Everly Strait, asked insightful questions of each young lady. Of course June knew her stuff.

Throughout the event, Sassy's focus never left the stage.

"Think you might want to do that one day?" Sam asked her.

"Yessir." Her bright eyes sparkled, then dimmed. "But I don't even know how to ride."

Sam glanced beyond her at Juliet. "Maybe we can do something about that."

"We'll see." Juliet hugged Sassy. "It's always fun to dream."

At last the competition finished, and Everly took center stage to crown the winner. When June's name wasn't announced for fourth, third, second or first place runner-up, the entire Mattson clan rose to cheer, drowning out his proclamation. "And your brand-new Miss Riverton Stampede for the coming year, Miss June Elizabeth Mattson!"

Nothing could have made Sam or his relatives prouder, especially her parents, Eli and Sue, and her brother, Eric. Whenever Sam felt down on life, he looked to Eric, injured four years before when the Brahman bull he was riding bucked him off and trampled him before the rodeo clowns could draw the bull away. Now in a wheelchair, Eric embodied faith, courage and resilience that set an example for the entire family.

After a celebration, Sam drove Juliet, Sassy and Jeff back to Miss Petra's ranch. "Get a good night of sleep, kids. We've got a lot to do tomorrow."

Sassy looked anything but sleepy as she danced into the house. Was she already dreaming about entering the competition for Miss Riverton Stampede? If Sam could help in any way, he'd be glad to do it. As for tomorrow, he looked forward to showing Jeff the event in which he and Raven would compete in the fall fair, plus taking an informative class in judging milk cows. This year's fair was turning out to be more fun than he'd had in years.

Juliet hadn't been to a fair since high school, so walking the midway and enjoying a few rides with Sam and the kids was as much a treat for her as for them. The Tilt-a-Whirl had her gasping and squealing as loudly as Sassy. And the aromas of barbecue, hot dogs and popcorn that filled the air incited her appetite. They all ate way more than they needed.

When Sam dropped a spot of mustard on his cambric shirt, Sassy teased him. "Mr. Sam, you sure are messy."

"Sure am." He winked at her before taking another bite.

Their short exchange sent warm feelings through Juliet. Some people would have been offended by a child's calling attention to their mishap. Not Sam.

They met up with Rob and Lauren's family, and Jeff and Sassy both knelt to pet Zoey's beautiful black-and-white companion dog, Lady. Sassy and Clementine greeted each other with girlish chatter, their blossoming friendship encouraging Juliet. Maybe that would help her daughter in school. Maybe when the truth came out about Sassy's paternity, as it surely would, Clementine would welcome her into the family as the cousin twice-removed that she was.

Jeff seemed particularly interested in the border collie. He ruffled her fur, and his eyes misted. Then he looked at Juliet and scowled as he always did when she caught him being emotional. Would she ever get to the bottom of that? Would he ever break down and talk about how their father dumped this border collie near Santa Fe and, more important, what happened when his mother died?

"Let's go see the pie judging." Sam waved a hand toward the large Cattlemen's Association exhibition hall where the various competitions were held. "After the judging, they sell the pies."

"Don't tell me you're still hungry after eating those hot dogs and fries." Juliet surprised herself with this light bit of teasing.

"I can always eat dessert," he said. "Besides, we Mattson men have hollow legs."

Sassy stared at Sam's jeans, then up at his face. "Does it hurt?"

Caught off guard, both Sam and Juliet burst into laughter. What a sweet moment of camaraderie. For a few seconds, Juliet wished it could last forever…before good sense took over.

"Silly kid." Jeff smirked at Sassy. "Ain't you ever heard

of a hollow leg? We Sizemore men have 'em, too. It just means we can eat as much as we want to without getting fat."

"Mom." Sassy jerked her gaze to Juliet. "Can we Sizemore girls do that, too?"

Juliet winced inwardly, remembering the cruel "more size" wordplay on her last name from some of the mean girls when she'd put on a few pounds from overeating during her parents' divorce. "Honey, it's never healthy or wise for anybody to eat too much."

After Rob's family moved on in a different direction, as if summoned by Juliet's unpleasant memories, Erin Farber and her daughter approached them. "Well, isn't this a cozy little group." She smirked. "Sam, I simply can't understand why you…"

Ginny leaned toward Sassy, her sugar-sweet sneer mirroring Erin's expression. "Your grandfather is a murderer."

Sassy gasped, her eyes filling with tears.

Juliet tugged her into a side hug. How could Erin teach her child to be so cruel? Before she could think of a response to protect Sassy, Jeff fisted his right hand and took a step toward the girl.

"You shut your—"

Sam grabbed his arm. "That doesn't solve anything. As for you, Erin, you disappoint me. Don't you ever ask yourself 'What would Jesus do?'"

"Well." Erin huffed. "You go ahead and eat with sinners." She raked Juliet and Jeff up and down with an arrogant stare. "Just don't expect decent people to do the same." She grabbed Ginny's hand and marched away.

If Sassy's tears weren't enough, Jeff's action terrified Juliet. Just like their father, he wanted to vent his anger on someone smaller and weaker. Never mind the child's cruel words.

"We want to go home." Jeff reached for Sassy's hand. "Come on, Jules."

"Hey, wait a minute." Sam clapped him on the shoulder. "We gotta find out if Miss Petra's peach cobbler won out over my mom's." He grinned as though they hadn't even encountered Erin and Ginny.

Jeff stared at him for several seconds. "But—"

"But nothing. Let's go support those good ladies." He made a big show of ushering them all toward the exhibition hall. "My mouth is already watering. How about you, Miss Juliet?"

At his playful tone, she half laughed, half sobbed. "Yeah. Me, too."

Not really, but she would go along with Sam's attempt to redeem the day. As he had back in high school, he'd stood up for a Sizemore. Only this time it was her daughter…and his. Best of all, he'd stopped Jeff from lashing out at Ginny, a desperate act that certainly could have landed him in juvie.

She might as well admit it, at least to herself. Sam Mattson was all she'd ever wanted in a man. If only she hadn't destroyed every chance of having a solid relationship with him by not telling him Sassy was his daughter. But that ship had sailed. No use trying to bring it back. He would only think she was still the liar she'd always been.

"Miss Petra, you're gonna have to give Mom your recipe." Sam polished off his dessert, then winked at Mom, who stood by the display table laden with various pies and other baked goods. "Your peach cobbler sure does deserve that blue ribbon."

"She sure does." Mom had the grace to nod her agreement with his compliment to her competition. He'd make it up to her later.

"Don't you be flattering me, Sam." Miss Petra wagged a finger at him. "Linda's cobbler is just as good, if not better. That Zeke Baldwin only gave me the blue ribbon because he wants to get on my good side. That's why he comes out to the ranch and buys hay from me for that old nag of his, so I'll go out with him."

"Is that so?" Sam laughed. "I don't blame Zeke. You're an attractive lady." *It runs in the family.* But he didn't dare say that out loud.

"Now don't you go on like that." Miss Petra's cheeks turned a little pink. "As for Zeke, if he wants to know me better, he should come to church."

"I won't argue with that." Sam glanced toward the picnic table where Juliet and the kids were eating tiny servings of several award-winning desserts. He lowered his voice and told Miss Petra and Mom about the unpleasant encounter with Erin and her daughter.

"Honestly, what is wrong with that woman?" Mom said.

Miss Petra sighed. "Seems to me she's never happy unless she's making somebody else *un*happy. Now, you go on over and join your fam…um, Juliet and the kids. Raeder's gonna take me home later."

Sam gave her a sidelong glance. She'd almost said "family." Why? And "the kids" weren't his, although he did feel responsible for them. He needed to be careful. Caring too much would only lead to another heartbreak. But somehow he almost felt like he'd been roped and wrangled into it. For some odd reason he couldn't explain even to himself, he wasn't resisting as much anymore.

"Hey, Miss Sassy." He ambled over to the table, where

she poked at the sweets on her paper plate, still wearing the wounded expression from Ginny's cruel remark. He plopped down on the bench beside her and nudged her with his arm. "Want to see some rabbits?"

Mild interest flickered in her eyes. "Rabbits?" She looked across the table at Juliet, whose frown indicated she hadn't recovered from Erin's attack either.

"Sure." Sam took in Jeff's scowl. "And after that, Jeff and I are taking a class on how to judge milk cows so he can see what Raven will need to win at the fall fair."

Jeff blinked, and his eyebrows rose. "We are?"

"You are?" Juliet's face brightened with appreciation. "That's great, isn't it, Jeff?"

For once the boy didn't shrug off an adult's suggestion. "Sounds cool. Let me finish this." He dug into his desserts.

Juliet gazed at Sam with…well, he wasn't quite sure how to describe her warm expression. Gratitude? No, more than that. Wait. Was she falling for him again? Maybe he needed to back off spending time with her. But somehow he couldn't break their shared gaze any more than she seemed able to do.

"Hey." Sassy punched his arm and let out a cross breath. "Why can't I learn how to judge milk cows?"

Sam forced his gaze away from Juliet and back to reality. Sassy loved her Uncle Jeff, but she also got jealous when he received more notice than she did. Maybe it was because of all those years when she'd had her mother's undivided attention.

"No reason you can't. Guess I just thought you'd rather meet up with Peanut and Raeder in the chicken-judging class."

"Well…" She scrunched up her cute little face as if

mulling over her choices. "Yeah, I want to see the chickens."

That settled, they made their way to the rabbit exhibition in another room. One blonde little girl was showing her large black rabbit to the judge, describing all the parts and how she took care of her bunny so he'd have that thick, shiny coat. In her record book open beside her, she displayed pictures of herself and her grandfather building a rabbit hutch as well as photos of the bunny's growth progress.

"What do you think, Sassy?" Sam eyed Juliet, whose gentle smile told him he was handling the situation right. "Would you rather raise rabbits or stick with your chickens?"

Basking in his attention, she grinned. "Rabbits are cute and cuddly, but so are chickens. And chickens lay eggs, so I'll stick with them."

Sam gave her an affirming nod. "Good plan. Just be sure to record everything in your record book, like Savannah's doing." Then to Juliet, "Now, about those eggs, don't forget—"

"I know." She rolled her eyes. "You get free eggs for a year. How could I forget?"

Her teasing tone struck something deep inside him. Before he could identify it, Jeff pointed to the clock over the entrance. "We gotta go. Our class starts in five minutes."

"Okay. Let's go." He waved to Juliet and Sassy. "See you girls later." And for him, later couldn't come soon enough.

The moment the guys walked away, Juliet faced the fact that she had to tell Sam about Sassy. Soon. Maybe tonight after he took them home. How could she deny it any longer, considering the way he'd already taken on a fatherly role in her daughter's life, even picking them up today to bring them out to the fair? She loved the way he noticed Sassy was jealous of Jeff and dealt with it gently. She loved the way he went far beyond Judge Mathis's orders and deeply involved himself in her brother's life. As they'd walked the midway and enjoyed the rides, they'd looked like any other family having a fun day at the fair. No, that was going too far. For now, she just had to tell Sam the truth and let the chips fall where they may. *Lord, please prepare his heart for this crushing news.* Because the last thing she wanted to do was break Sam Mattson's heart again. The more she thought about it, she wanted to take care of that tender heart with all of hers.

As important as the class was for Jeff's 4-H project, Sam sensed the boy needed to talk about what happened with Erin and her daughter. Seated at the back of the large exhibition hall where the heifers were on display and the expert gave his lecture, Jeff seemed to have lost his earlier interest. Instead, he stared down at his interlocked hands and chewed his lower lip. Sam decided to tackle it head-on.

"You want to talk about what happened with Sassy's classmate?"

Jeff jerked his head up, revealing reddened eyes. "Sam, I almost hit that little brat. I would have if you hadn't stopped me." Misery and horror were written across his face. He stared down again. "I-I'm glad you did."

Holding on to his emotions, Sam nodded. "Yeah. Me, too."

Jeff brushed a hand over his eyes. "I'm just like my father. Maybe it was my fault Mom died."

"What? No, don't let him get to you that way." Sam

searched for words to console him. "Listen, your original testimony to the cops is exactly what happened. Forensics proved it. And for the record, I spoke to both Sheriff Blake and Deputy Northam, and they said nobody smelled alcohol on your breath that night. Dill was just trying to get into your head and confuse you." He paused. "Look, I know he's your dad, and you want his approval. His love. But Dill Sizemore is—"

"A sleazebag." Jeff snorted out a bitter laugh. "Might as well say it. I'm not proud of him."

"Hey, we all want to admire our dads." Sam set a hand on Jeff's shoulder. "It's good you don't want to follow in Dill's footsteps. Jesus can help you not to do that. When our earthly parents disappoint us, if we trust in Jesus as our Savior, we have a heavenly Father who loves us and won't let us down. Jesus will step in and be the Father you need. Just ask Him."

"That's what Bobby said." Jeff scoffed. "But he's got a great dad, so what does he know?"

"Yes, Rob's a good dad, but he and Bobby don't always see eye to eye." Sam considered telling Jeff about his own years of rebellion. Maybe later. Right now Jeff was trying to divert the attention away from the only lasting solution to his own problems. Time to get him back on track. "Just remember. Jesus can help you with self-control so you don't have to give in to a violent temper like your dad did." *And still does.* Sam had learned about some brawls Dill had been involved in at the prison, not the wisest behavior for a man trying to beat a manslaughter charge.

"I'll think about it." Jeff exhaled a long breath. "I want to tell my dad to his face that he's not gonna blame me for Ma's death. Like you said, I saw what I saw, just like I told the cops." He looked at Sam, determination in his eyes. "Will you take me? Not with Juliet. Just me and you?"

Sam considered the idea. He didn't like it. But Jeff confronting Dill with the truth about Brenda's death might build some much needed confidence in the boy. Sam did like the idea of not including Juliet in the visit. She sure didn't need to endure more hurt from their dad.

"I'll check with Judge Mathis."

"Thanks." Jeff slid a wily look his way. "You know who else needs a good dad?" He grinned and nudged Sam. "Sassy."

Sam tried not to squirm in his seat. Vague images of the faceless man who'd fathered Sassy spun through his mind.

"I don't know what's wrong with my dumb sister. Why doesn't she just tell you the truth?"

Sam's heart seemed to stop beating. "Wh-what truth?"

Jeff snorted. "You mean you haven't figured it out yet? I did even before I found Sass's birth certificate. What are you, a birdbrain when it comes to my sister?"

Sam thought his head might explode. Before he spoke, he swallowed hard. "Go on."

Now Jeff laughed. "Come on, Sam. Just think about it. Who else could be her dad but you? We call her Sassy, but her real name is Samantha Anne Sizemore. *Sam*antha? Grab a clue, *Sam*. She was named after you."

No. It can't be. Sam coughed away the nausea trying to rise in his throat. If a knife were stabbed into his heart, it couldn't hurt more than this revelation. "Uh..." He swallowed the pain-filled groan trying to escape him.

"So, *brother*." Jeff injected his words with a sarcastic tone. "Why don't you ask my sister to marry you? You have my permission. Then you can be the dad Sassy needs."

Sam managed a weak chuckle, more like a cough. "We'd

better get back to the girls. I promised them we'd ride the Ferris wheel."

He stood and walked toward the door, not bothering to check if Jeff was following. If what he said was true, this changed everything. All of his kind feelings toward Juliet soured. She'd always been a liar, and she'd been living a lie since coming back to Riverton. He'd have to do a lot of praying before he could forgive her for denying him the right to be a father to his own daughter all these years.

"Mom, do you like Mr. Sam?" Sassy repeated a question she'd asked several times before.

"Yes, I still like Mr. Sam." Juliet took Sassy's hand as they navigated the crowd emerging from the chicken-judging class. It had often occurred to her that she needed to prepare Sassy for the news that Sam was her dad. "Do you like him?"

"Uh-huh. And I think he likes us, too." Sassy gave her a mischievous grin. "So why don't you marry him?"

Caught off guard, Juliet gaped. "What? Where did you get such an idea?"

Sassy shrugged. "Clementine said she got a new mom when Mr. Rob married Miss Lauren." Her expression turned shy. "If you married Mr. Sam, I could have a dad."

A familiar ache opened in Juliet's heart. "It's complicated, sweetheart."

Before she could say more, Sassy broke away. "There's Jeffie and Mr. Sam." She ran to greet them.

Juliet's heart did another turn. When they got home tonight, would she have the courage to tell Sam the truth? From the scowl on his face, she shut down that thought. What on earth?

"Ready to ride the Ferris wheel?" Jeff grabbed Sassy's hand. "Let's go."

He and Sassy jogged toward the towering ride.

"Wow, he really sounds excited." Juliet chuckled. "I wonder if he's ever ridden one before. Dill wasn't much into taking us kids out for fun."

"Figures." Hands jammed in his jeans pockets, Sam walked beside her.

"Is something wrong?" Once again, Juliet's heart flipped unpleasantly.

"Wrong?" Sam huffed. "Not with me."

They reached the ticket booth, and Sam grimaced as he purchased four rides. Once they were secured in the seats across from the kids in the four-person passenger cab, he appeared to scoot as far from Juliet as he could. Jeff, on the other hand, looked like the cat that got the cream. What had he done to make Sam so cross? Or maybe she was the one.

As the giant wheel started upward, she tried to gulp down her queasiness so Sassy wouldn't catch on to her fear of heights. This morning when she agreed to ride this monstrosity, she'd assumed Sam would calm her fears. But now he clearly didn't want any part of her. Sassy was another matter. When they reached the top, the wheel stopped, the cab swayed, and she squealed with both fright and delight. Sam pointed toward something in the distance.

"Hey, Sassy." His voice caught oddly. Was he scared, too? "Look over there. You can see the mountains. They still have snowcaps."

The diversion worked. "And look." Sassy pointed to the paragliders flying over the high school football field. "Mom, can we do that next?"

"You can't paraglide, Squirt." Jeff looked a little green,

but he was bravely hanging in there. "You're so little, you'd blow away to Colorado, and we'd never find you."

"Would not." Sassy stared around them, calling their attention to other distant sights, the only one in the cab who seemed to be enjoying herself.

As for Sam's sullenness, it caused Juliet's stomach to churn with nausea that had nothing to do with the sudden jolt of the Ferris wheel as it resumed its circular trip. After the ride finally ended, she had no trouble agreeing with him that they should call it a day and go home.

What had happened between him and Jeff during their cow-judging class? If she weren't dependent on him for a ride, if she didn't know that once they reached the ranch she had to tell him the truth about Sassy, she would have reminded him of his promise to take them to tonight's concert. But the anticipated enjoyment of hearing her favorite country and western singers paled in importance to finally telling Sam the truth.

Chapter Thirteen

As Juliet, Sassy and Jeff climbed out of his pickup, Sam couldn't bring himself to follow them into the house even though she'd invited him in for coffee. He also couldn't bring himself to drive away. He should confront Juliet right now. He put his hand on the door handle at the same moment she reemerged from the house, so he climbed out to meet her.

"You sure you don't want that coffee?" Her vulnerable expression came close to softening his anger, but didn't quite make it.

"We can talk right here." He jutted his chin toward the house. "So when were you going to tell me about Sassy?"

She blinked in that way of hers that usually melted away any angry feelings. Not this time. "You mean that she's your daughter?"

He scoffed. "So it's true. In spite of…" He couldn't say the words. Obviously, the foolish advice about "precautions" from his teenage buddies hadn't worked. What a numbskull he'd been…and still was.

"Yes, she's your daughter." A hint of defensiveness crossed her eyes, replaced quickly by sadness. "How did you figure it out?"

"I didn't. Jeff said he found her birth certificate naming me as her father." He exhaled a harsh breath. "So her real name is Samantha."

"Oh, that brother of mine. I should have known he'd snoop around the house." She gave him a chagrined look. "So, yes. I named her after you. Of course."

Sam turned away and ran a hand down the back of his neck, then looked at her again. "Why didn't you tell me you were pregnant? Why didn't you just meet me like we planned so we could elope? All these years, I could have taken care of you…"

"I know." Now her tears started, but he refused to let them get to him. "Don't you remember how hard those times were for me? My folks were divorced, and like every kid, I was desperate to win my dad's affection. Mama figured out that I was pregnant and told Dad. I don't know how he found out we planned to elope, but he locked me in the spare bedroom at his house so I couldn't meet you that night. He told Mama to tell the school and her friends that I'd left town, then kept me there until the school year ended. He also wanted me to, well, not be pregnant. I would have done anything to get his approval, but not that."

Such a fragile thread had led to Sassy's birth. As Sam considered the possible alternative, nausea once again rose up in his throat. "Go on."

"That's when Mama said I should actually leave town before he could force me to do it. She arranged for me to go live with one of her relatives in Alamosa to have the baby, then give her up for adoption. Dill said okay as long as it didn't cost him anything. Mama scraped together the money, and off I went. But I wouldn't give Sassy up either. My cousin babysat her while I earned my GED and a pre-vet science degree at Adams State University. I worked hard and earned it in three years." She emitted an ironic laugh. "I further got on Dad's nerves by naming Sassy after you. That really made him mad. When we went to the prison last month, I was afraid he was going to tell you about her, but he probably was waiting for a chance to use the truth to hurt you…or blackmail me."

So this was what Dill had referred to.

"That's just the thing, Juliet. Why didn't *you* tell me?" He couldn't keep the anger from his voice. "And you let some relative you barely knew help you raise our daughter instead of trusting me to help you? Do you have any idea how much that hurts? All these wasted years…"

"Sam, you're being unreasonable." Eyes blazing, she posted her fists at her waist.

"Unreasonable?" Sam ground his teeth. "Because of your decisions, I missed out on nine years of my d-daughter's life." He could barely get the word out.

"What part of my being locked in a bedroom at his house did you not hear? He took away my phone. By the time Mama talked him into letting me go to Alamosa, you'd already left for college."

Sam tried to generate some understanding of her situation, but the knife-sharp pain in his chest would not let him. "Why wouldn't Brenda help you?"

"She never dared to cross him. Look at what it got her when she finally did."

Good sense told Sam that Juliet had indeed been trapped. But anger overrode any sympathy trying to take root in his heart. "Once he let you out, you could have called me."

"What? Ask your parents where you'd gone to school? Ask them for your phone number? Ask the almighty Mattson family to acknowledge my child? Before I left, your mother wouldn't even say hello to me when we bumped into each other in the supermarket. I couldn't wait to get out of town." She let out an angry breath. "Every so-called decent person in Riverton thinks every Sizemore is trash. How could a golden boy like you ever understand what that's like?"

Golden boy? Maybe. He couldn't deny he'd been treated like one even though he'd hated it. "But that was the whole thing about us being attracted to each other. We were rebelling against a hundred and forty or fifty years of a stupid feud between our families." Sam tried to stop, but his angry words kept coming. "Or maybe it wasn't so stupid. Back then, Jeb Sizemore lied about his cattle rustling, and all these generations later, your father is still a liar. I guess the apple doesn't fall far from the tree. Like your father and every other Sizemore, you were never good friends with the truth. You lived a lie by not telling me you were pregnant. You lied to Rob about Lauren and his stolen dog. And you've been living a lie since you came back to town by not telling me Sassy is my child. I never should have trusted you."

Before he said something worse, Sam jerked open his truck door and climbed in. Through the windshield, he saw Sassy and Jeff standing by the back door, Sassy sobbing and Jeff glaring at him. It hurt to see them so upset. But he didn't trust himself to try to fix the mess Juliet had caused by her omission of the truth and her outright lies.

"Wait!" Juliet ran to his side window.

Reluctantly, he pressed the button to let it down. "What?"

"I-I still need you to be Jeff's co-guardian, at least until the end of the school year. And I was hoping you'd agree to stay until Dill's trial is over." Her tearstained face was bright red, from anger or embarrassment, he didn't care which. "Please."

He turned away so her pleading couldn't move him. "I have never in my life reneged on a promise, personally or professionally. I won't start now." And yet, how could he continue to help Sassy and Jeff with their 4-H projects? The idea of breaking his promises to them sent a new ache through his heart. But he'd have to sort that out later. Right now, he couldn't get away from Juliet fast enough.

Shame, anger and fear warred within Juliet as she watched Sam drive away. Why had she ever gone to the Mattson law offices to ask for help with Jeff? With the way her life usually went, of course Will wouldn't be in the office that day, so she'd been stuck with Sam.

The sound of Sassy's sobs broke through her useless musing. She hurried to the back door, where Jeff was trying to console her daughter.

"What a jerk." Jeff scowled. "I'm sorry, Sis. I never should have told him."

"It's not your fault, Jeff. I planned to tell him tonight anyway." She would scold him later about his snooping through her personal papers.

"Is he my daddy?" Sassy stared up at Juliet through tear-filled eyes.

Juliet pulled her into her arms. "Yes, sweetheart. I'm sorry I didn't tell you sooner."

"I don't like him anymore." She brushed a hand over her damp cheeks. "He was mean to you."

"Well, he didn't know…" Why was she defending him?

"We'll get by, kid." Jeff gently tugged Sassy's ponytail. "I'll look out for you. Like I always say, we Sizemores gotta stick together."

Although that old saying had always made Juliet's stomach turn, considering Dill's abusive treatment of his family, it might be closer to the truth than her brother realized. At least she and her family, and Mama, could be counted on to stick together. She hoped.

After a light supper none of them wanted to eat, Juliet put Sassy to bed and reminded Jeff to do his homework. "You've been doing so good, Jeff. Don't let Sam's behavior knock you off track."

A moment of confusion passed over his face. Then he nodded. "I won't. Just because he's a creep to you doesn't mean he hasn't done some okay stuff for us. Me and you can take it from here as long as we stick together."

His words echoed her own thoughts. For the first time since Sam turned on her this afternoon, Juliet felt a ray of light in her heart. Maybe Jeff was finally getting past his troubles and taking responsibility for his actions. As Mama would say, the Lord was working it out.

Raeder brought Mama home, then took sleepy little Peanut to their home in the bunkhouse. With her usual discerning ways, Mama didn't take long to dig out the details about Sam.

"Honey, you'll have to forgive me for saying this, but I told you to tell him. He's a decent man. Look at everything he's done for you and the kids." Looking weary from her long day, she unpacked her baking dish and utensils from her canvas carryall, which was decorated with her bright blue ribbon, and set them in the sink. "He'll cool down and sort this out with you."

"Sort what out, Mama? We were finished before we even got started. And I'm sure not going to ask him for anything. He promised to help with Jeff, but he doesn't have to do anything more for Sassy." She squirted soap into the dish and added hot tap water. "I'll clean up. You go on to bed." She scrubbed at the baked-on remnants of peach cobbler.

"You sure you don't want to talk some more?" Mama chuckled softly. "Here's a man who works in family law trying to rebuild broken families, and he didn't even know he had one of his own." Another chuckle. "You may not have any choice about what he does for Sassy. New Mexico law doesn't look kindly on deadbeat dads. I learned that with Dill when he refused to pay child support for you. The judge forced him to. Threatened jail time if he didn't. Besides, you surely don't think Sam Mattson won't take responsibility for his own child? Now that he knows about her, I mean?"

Juliet rinsed the dish and set it in the drain rack, then dried her hands on a tea towel. "Go to bed, Mama. I still have to get up early for work." School was out because of the fair, so the kids could sleep in. That would make Juliet's morning a little less complicated than usual.

Mama pulled her into a strong hug. "I'll be praying for you. And for Sam. Try to think of what this looks like to him. He must be devastated."

After Mama went to bed, Juliet sat at the kitchen table and sipped Sleepytime tea. Maybe the tea would help her overcome the painful thoughts whirling through her brain like the Tilt-a-Whirl they'd ridden just a few hours ago. Mama had been right all along, of course. She should have told Sam the truth. Even when she'd prayed about it, she'd felt the urge to do so. Yet her lifelong stubbornness, another destructive Sizemore family trait, had kept her hanging on to the truth so she could maintain some sort of control. But where had that gotten her? Why hadn't she listened to Mama and, even more important, the Lord's prompting? When would she ever learn? Most of all, how could she maintain some semblance of a relationship with Sam for Jeff's sake? His unforgiving attitude would make it difficult, as would his shouting at her. She wouldn't go through that again.

To think she'd actually begun to dream of them all becoming a family. What a foolish flight of fancy. She didn't even know what a happy family was. Or what a happy marriage was. Her parents' divorce had wounded her badly.

She had to stop this. It was too late for such musings. One thing she knew for sure: she'd been forgiven by the Lord, so she refused to live in shame. As soon as Dad's trial was over, she would take Jeff and Sassy someplace far away where nobody had ever heard of the Sizemore–Mattson feud.

He was a father. How had he not figured that out? All these years he could have been loving Sassy and helping her grow up a Mattson and without the stigma of her mother's infamous last name. Never mind that making a family with Juliet at eighteen could have prevented him from earning his degrees and subsequent law career. But those nine years of missing out on his daughter's life broke his heart.

With the truth out in the open and sure to spread rapidly all around Riverton and the county, as soon as he arrived home, he sat his parents down for a long overdue chat. Make that a long overdue *confession*.

"Oh, Sam." Mom's tears were accompanied by a big smile. "This is such good news. It's everything I hoped and prayed for."

"Good news?" He stared at her. "You mean you hoped and prayed for me to have a child outside of marriage?"

"Not that, son." Dad, with his usual calm demeanor, gave Sam a rueful smile. "But when we saw how you and Juliet were managing a difficult situation with Jeff—"

"And we saw your obvious affection for Sassy and Juliet." Mom dabbed at her nose with a tissue. "We've noticed how Juliet has blossomed in her faith and what a good mother she is. Why do you think we invited them over for dinner that Sunday?"

"So you suspected Sassy's my daughter?" Somehow the words came out a little easier this time.

"Not at all, dear." Mom shook her head. "We assumed, as you did, that Juliet had had another boyfriend." She winced. "I'm ashamed of myself for judging her so harshly all those years ago. One of these days, I hope she will forgive me."

"We understood your teenage rebellion, son," Dad said. "It's not easy to grow up a Mattson with all the expectations put on us."

"But you were too young to marry back then." Mom gave him a scolding look. "Or to engage in for-marriage-only activities."

Heat rose up Sam's neck. He'd never talked about such things with his folks, especially not Mom. "She should have told me she was expecting. Or when she came back to town earlier this year. Why couldn't she just tell me then that Sassy's my daughter?" For the first time since Jeff broke the news to him, Sam felt a kick of excitement. He had a daughter!

"Oh, Andy, we have our first grandchild!" Mom clutched her hands to her chest. "Oh, if I could just hug her right now. I am officially over the moon with happiness!"

"It'd be a big shame if you won't let us be part of Sassy's life." Dad's blue eyes misted. "You need to go back to Juliet and tell her you forgive her."

"Ahem!" Mom chided them both with a frown. "And ask her to forgive you for your angry outburst at her."

"Who knows—" Dad put on his Sunday school teacher face "—Sassy might just be the key to putting an end to that old Mattson–Sizemore feud."

"Ha!" Sam scoffed. "Don't put that responsibility on a little kid, especially not my daughter." The more often he said it, the more he loved the idea. He ran a hand over the newly upholstered arm of his chair. "But thanks for your help. It never occurred to me how happy you'd be at having a grandchild."

"What?" Mom laughed. "You and Sadie haven't gotten the message yet? Of course we want grandchildren. And the more the merrier."

"At least Sadie's engaged to that big city lawyer," Dad said. "Now, you get back over to the Murphy ranch and make up with Juliet so we can officially welcome Sassy into the family."

"Dad, it's ten o'clock."

"Well, then, first thing in the morning." He sounded all too authoritarian, much like he had when Sam was a teen. "You get this straightened out so we can start spoiling our Sassy."

Oddly, Sam didn't mind his stern tone. In fact, having his parents' blessing, he was free to explore his own heart. He'd been fond of Sassy from the start, and over these past few months, Jeff had also claimed a piece of his heart. Maybe it was time to truly explore his feelings for Juliet. That was, if she would forgive him for his angry words.

"You're up early." Juliet greeted Jeff as he set two buckets of milk on the mudroom table. "Did you forget there's no school today? And when did you start milking in the morning?"

"Just want to help Raeder out by milking one of the cows." He gave her a sheepish grin. "Like we said last night, we gotta stick together, and Raeder seems more than just our cowhand. He's part of the family."

His words encouraged Juliet. "I'm so proud of you, little brother." If not for the remaining sting in her chest from yesterday's confrontation with Sam, she'd burst with happiness over Jeff's improvements. To his credit, he didn't seem to expect perfection from her or from Sam before cleaning up his act. "On the other hand, maybe we should have a few lessons in not snooping into other people's private papers."

"Yeah, well." Another sheepish grin. "Sorry for stealing your thunder yesterday."

"Thunder?" She rolled her eyes. "The only thunder yesterday was Sam's." Guilt and sorrow stung her at the memory of the hurt in his eyes.

"Jeff, did Sassy go out to milk with you?" Still in her robe and slippers, Mama entered the kitchen.

"What?" Juliet's heart seemed to stand still. "Isn't she in her bed?"

"No," Mama answered on a sob.

"Miss Petra?" Raeder called from outside the mudroom door. "Miss Juliet?"

"Come on in." Jeff opened the door for him.

"Have you seen Peanut?" Raeder's face was ashen beneath his tan. "I didn't check on him before I went out to milk, and when I did, his bed was empty."

A new kind of fear swept through Juliet. "Sassy's not here, either."

"Where could they be?" Mama cried. "Dear Lord, please don't let them be kidnapped."

"Now, ma'am, let's don't panic." Despite his words, Raeder looked on the verge of panic himself. "They've got to be hiding here someplace. Jeff, do you know where they usually play hide-and-go-seek?"

"Yessir. Out by the chicken coop. Maybe they're checking on the chicks after taking that class yesterday."

They all dashed across the barnyard toward the chicken yard, then searched every corner of the barn. The children were nowhere to be found, and Juliet had never felt such paralyzing fear in her life.

"I'm going to call the sheriff." Mama pulled out her cell phone. "Rex. Petra Murphy here. Listen, my granddaughter and little Peanut Westfall have gone missing." Pause. "Yes, we've searched everyplace on the ranch." Another pause. "Oh, thank you. Thank you." She punched her phone. "He's rustling up a search party and sending out the word to all his deputies. Somebody'll be here soon."

"Come on, Jeff." His face a resolute mask, Raeder headed toward his Bronco. "We'll drive up the road and see if they went that way. They couldn't have gotten far."

"I'm coming, too." Juliet followed them.

"Ma'am, I think you'd best stay here so you can talk to the deputies."

"That's a good idea, Raeder." Mama grasped Juliet's arm. "Before you go, let's make a circle and pray."

Even Jeff joined hands with them, which at any other time, would have thrilled Juliet. This morning, her fear overrode every other emotion and concern.

"Dear Lord, we love You," Mama prayed, "and we love these kids. You know where they are. Please bring them back home safely. In Jesus's name. Amen."

The others, even Jeff, chorused "amen."

Other than when Juliet had asked Jesus to save her, she had never sent up a more desperate plea to the Almighty in her life.

"Hey, Sam." Deputy Cameron Northam spoke in a somber tone in his early morning phone call. "You gonna join the search for those lost kids?"

"Lost kids?" Sam's heart seemed to stop beating as he shook off sleep. "Who—"

"The Sizemore girl and Westfall's kid." Cameron's impatience came through, like Sam was supposed to have heard about this.

"What happened?" Foolish question. Sassy's tears yesterday should have warned him she would react like a Sizemore and do something rash. Instantly he regretted his judgment. Mattsons were known to do a few rash things, too.

"No idea. Just know they've gone missing. You gonna help?"

"Yeah. Of course. Where should I go?"

"We're meeting up at the Murphy ranch as soon as possible."

"I'll be right there."

Not bothering to shave, Sam threw on yesterday's jeans and shirt, complete with mustard stain, and headed downstairs.

"Where you going, son?" Dad was working on a cup of coffee.

"Sassy's gone missing, along with Peanut Westfall." Sam grabbed a travel cup and poured coffee for himself. "They're gathering a search party over at Petra's place and—"

"Say no more." Dad set aside his coffee and strode across the kitchen to grab his Stetson from the hat rack by the back door. "What are you waiting for?"

As the sun crested the distant mountains, they each climbed into their own vehicles and headed out. Sam autodialed Mom to let her know about the kids, only to learn Dad had beat him to it. Of course. His folks were always on the same wavelength. He had no doubt Mom wouldn't be far behind them.

Pulling into the lane to Petra's ranch behind Dad, Sam saw a long line of trucks parking near the house and barn. He should have known the community would come together to find missing kids…even if one of them was a Sizemore. Guilt and fear gnawed at Sam's gut. If only… if only…

He found a place to park his truck among the many volunteers. Even Rob was there with one of his new search dogs. Sam jumped out and jogged over to Juliet and Miss Petra, who were huddled with Sheriff Rex Blake and Deputy Cameron Northam in the center of the crowd of volunteers. Juliet saw him coming and ran to meet him. Then stopped abruptly.

"Thank you for coming." Suddenly formal?

"Of course I came. Sassy's my daughter, and if I—"

"Right. If only you'd known that from the start, this wouldn't have happened." She spun around and walked away.

"Juliet!" He caught up with her and touched her shoulder.

She whirled around and glared up at him. "What?"

"I'm here to help. We can settle the past once we find her. And Peanut. Poor little guy."

Now her tears came, and Sam was helpless against

them. He gently tugged Juliet into his arms. "We'll find them, Jules."

"If only she'd talked to me." She pulled back, her eyes pleading. "I'm sorry for not telling you about her."

"I'm sorry I didn't realize your father would trap you. I should have tried to find out why you didn't come to meet me."

"Miss Juliet." Rex beckoned to her. "We've got a plan. Everybody has their orders." He indicated the trucks heading toward the highway. "We don't think the kids were kidnapped, but just to be sure, we've asked the highway patrol to set up roadblocks."

"How can you be sure nobody took them?" Even as he said the words, Sam felt another wave of nausea.

"Peanut butter." Miss Petra stepped up beside Rex. "When I went back inside a bit ago, I found open jars of peanut butter and jelly and a loaf of bread on the kitchen counter. And half of my last batch of cookies are gone. Sassy must have made a snack for her...for her—" She stopped on a sob.

"And her backpack is gone." Juliet put her arm around her mother. "Along with her favorite stuffed bear."

Pictures of cartoon runaways—with all their belongings tied in a bundle on a stick flung over their shoulders—flashed through Sam's mind, but this was all too real and not the least bit cute or funny. "Where would she go? And why would she take Peanut with her so early in the morning?"

"Maybe he saw her leaving and she took him along to keep him from telling on her?" Rex gave Juliet a questioning look.

"I don't know." She shrugged. "What can I do?"

"Best for you and Miss Petra to stay here. Could be the

kids will come back. Could be they're hiding in the bushes someplace around the ranch." He waved a hand toward Rob and his search dog moving into the scrub grass with other volunteers. "So far his dog hasn't picked up the scent of either kid past the barn and bunkhouse. That's why we're mainly focusing on the highway."

Sam considered several possibilities. "Miss Petra, would any of your customers come by for milk before sunup?" He nodded toward the back porch refrigerator, where folks could pick up gallons of milk and leave payment on the honor system.

"Not today. I checked the fridge, and last night's milking is still there." Her brow furrowed. "Can't think of anybody else who'd come around that early. Well, other than Zeke Baldwin. He comes out and gets hay from time to time. When it's early, he doesn't bother to tell me, just puts a check in the mailbox. But Zeke wouldn't take the kids. Got grandkids of his own."

Rex shifted his stance impatiently. "Do you know if he came out this morning for hay?"

"How would I know?" Miss Petra scowled at him. "I don't count my hay bales, and I haven't been to the mailbox yet."

"But, ma'am—" Rex blew out a breath "—he might have seen the kids. Might have seen a strange vehicle—"

"Oh, I should have thought of that." Miss Petra burst into tears again.

Juliet hugged her again. "Me, too, Mama." She looked over Miss Petra's shoulder at Sam. "Can you call Zeke?"

"Well, he doesn't have a cell phone," Miss Petra said. "Refuses to come into the modern age." She punched a number into her own phone. "No answer at his house."

"I'll check the mailbox, then drive over there." Sam patted Miss Petra's shoulder and nodded to Juliet. As much as he wanted to give her another reassuring hug, her cross expression warned him off. What had happened in the few minutes since they'd shared that embrace? For him, it had felt like a breakthrough. For her, obviously not.

"I'm going with you." Juliet followed him to his truck and climbed in.

"Didn't Rex want you to stay here with your mom?"

"I'm going with you." This time, she growled out the words.

As he had back in high school, Sam knew that when she made up her mind, he should just give up trying to change it. Driving up the road toward the highway, he saw Mom coming the other way. Good. She could keep Miss Petra company. They traded waves as they stopped by the mailbox. It was empty.

"It's good of your folks to come out and help." Juliet stared out the opposite window.

"Of course. They're as worried about their granddaughter as I am."

She jerked her attention to him. "You told them?"

"Sure did." Despite their desperate situation, he couldn't resist a chuckle. "They can't wait to formally welcome her to the family."

For some strange reason, that announcement caused Juliet to burst into tears again.

Chapter Fourteen

Juliet hadn't cried this hard in years. Life had taught her tears did nothing to solve problems. But when it came to Sassy, her emotions all too easily spilled out. Why did it have to be in front of Sam? Oh, how she hated for him to see her weaknesses. Unlike their long-ago romance, such as it was, she could not, would not trust him now with her deepest feelings.

She shot him a quick glance, but his eyes were on the highway as they sped toward Zeke Baldwin's ranch some ten miles away. With school out for the fair, traffic was lighter than usual, so she appreciated his sense of urgency in exceeding the speed limit.

"I can't figure out why little Peanut is missing, too." Sam's words broke into her thoughts.

She brushed her tears away and inhaled a deep breath. "Haven't you noticed how he follows her around like a little puppy?" She almost smiled at the picture that brought to mind.

"Yeah. That's pretty cute." He chuckled. "I guess he can tell she can be trusted."

She stared at his profile for a moment, longing to say, "she learned that from me," but not daring to open a door that would only lead to another accusation and more pain. "Yes. Right up until today."

"Now don't be going in that direction." He spared her a quick look. "Once we find them, she'll give us some wise-in-a-nine-year-old's-way-of-thinking explanation."

"Sounds like you know kids." She had to admit he'd engaged with Sassy better than the average adult. But that was before he knew…

"We see lots of them in our family law practice. Most kids just want to be loved. To be secure." His voice caught. "I want Sassy to have that, too." His expression turned vulnerable. "Whatever it takes, I want to be part of her life…if you'll let me."

She wanted to say yes, but the word stuck in her throat. Letting Sam be a dad to Sassy meant she could lose control of her daughter's life and future. Letting Linda and Andy be involved as Sassy's grandparents would further erode her control. Being swept up into the vast Mattson clan could cause both her and Sassy to lose their identities. But who were they? Daughter and granddaughter of a murderer. But also Mama's kin, and she was the best example of a Christian Juliet had ever known. What had she advised? Tell Sam he had a daughter.

Okay, she would tell him he could be part of Sassy's life. That was, if they found her.

Before she could say the words, his car phone buzzed and a caller ID flashed on the screen. He punched the button on the dash. "Greg, what's up?"

"Sam, is Juliet Sizemore with you?"

"Yeah. Right here on speaker."

"I'm here." Juliet shot Sam a cross look. She could answer for herself.

"Miss Sizemore, this is Greg Mattson over at the train

station." He chuckled. "There's a little package for you down here. And one for Raeder. I'm gonna call him next."

"Thank You, Lord." Sam laughed with relief. "How on earth did they get clear to the train station?" He put on his blinker and flipped a U-turn to head back toward town.

Juliet gulped back her own sob of relief. Of course it was a Mattson who found the kids. They were everywhere. Did Greg, the stationmaster, already know Sassy was one of them? Did everybody know? Once again she wanted to grab her daughter and Jeff and leave this town forever. But where could she take them where the long-armed tentacles of the Mattson clan couldn't reach Sassy and pull her into their controlling grasp, complete with who knew what expectations she could never live up to?

Sam drove into the parking lot of the newly renovated brick Riverton Train Station and found an open space near the entrance. Outside on the platform, travelers and baggage awaited the next train. Through the large picture window, Sam could see his middle-aged, red-haired Cousin Greg in his dark blue uniform, arms crossed, a stern expression on his face, and talking to someone much shorter. Only the top of Sassy's blond hair was visible, but from Greg's stance, he was obviously scolding more than one little person. Or pointing out the dangers of being close to the train tracks without adult supervision. Greg had put the fear of danger into countless runaways.

Juliet hopped out of the truck and ran inside, with Sam close behind.

"Samantha Anne Sizemore!" Juliet's stern address made both kids jump. "What are you doing here?"

Sassy ran to her open arms, sobbing. "I'm sorry, Mommy."

Though he felt like an outsider in this reunion, relief flooded Sam's entire being, and he emitted a quiet laugh. He'd noticed from the start that Sassy called Juliet "Mommy" whenever she felt vulnerable or when she wanted to avoid trouble. He'd seen that in many children. No matter their ages, in moments of crisis, kids usually wanted to cling to their parents.

As for little Peanut, he was hugging his stuffed giraffe and sucking his thumb, his brown eyes wide as he watched Sassy and Juliet's reunion. Yet he didn't seem particularly upset or concerned, even when Raeder ran into the station with Jeff.

"Hey, little buddy, where you been?" Eyes red, Raeder knelt and lifted his tiny son into his arms.

"Daddy, we went on the hay truck." He spoke as if he'd just ridden a merry-go-round.

"You did?" Deep affection filled Raeder's face. He shot a look at Juliet and Sassy. "That must have been fun."

"Uh-huh." Peanut's thumb went back in his mouth.

"Care to explain yourself, missy?" Juliet held Sassy's shoulders and stared into her eyes. "What's this about a hay truck?"

Whimpering, Sassy shrugged and looked down.

"You know you have to answer me. So, spill it!"

Juliet's firmness stirred up Sam's admiration. She was a good mother, no doubt about it. Some parents he'd dealt with made excuses for their kids, no matter how bad their behavior.

"Well, I… I was mad at you and Mr. Sam. Jeffie said you made a mistake and I was born—"

"Jeff!" Juliet gasped.

"Wait. No. Sass, that's not what I meant." Jeff appeared as close to tears as his sister and niece. He tugged her away from Juliet and hugged her. "Everybody loves you, Sass.

You're the heart of our family." He glanced at Sam. "And Sam's family, too."

"Absolutely." Sam nodded. This was progress for Jeff.

Sassy turned toward Sam, hurt and disappointment radiating from her eyes. All the experience and training in the world couldn't prescribe how he should respond. He had only his heart to guide him.

He sat on a bench and took Sassy's hands, drawing her to sit beside him. "Sweetheart, I'm so glad you were born. I'm so glad you're my daughter." His voice broke on the word *daughter*. He swallowed hard, then stage-whispered, "Not many people know this, but we lawyers don't usually hang out at 4-H meetings and county fairs with their clients." He winked. "But I've had more fun with you and Jeff than I've had in a long time." At her tearful half smile, he maintained a playful tone. "Now, what's this about riding on a hay truck? How'd you manage that?"

She gave him an impish grin. "Mr. Zeke didn't know we climbed up behind the hay bales at Gramma's. He got all the way to town and didn't see us. So we climbed down when he parked at the hardware store." She glanced beyond Sam at Greg, who still stood there with arms crossed, the famous Mattson grin on his face, obviously enjoying all of this family drama. Behind the counter, gray-haired Mrs. Hurst from church focused her eyes on a computer screen, but her nearest ear seemed lifted a little higher so she could hear every word.

Juliet had also been watching Sassy's exchange with Sam, but her expression was guarded, almost as if she suddenly didn't trust him with their daughter.

"We were gonna take the train to Santa Fe to my old house." Sassy spoke as if this was perfectly logical, as Sam had expected.

"What!" Juliet sat down on Sassy's other side. "Why on earth would you go there? You know we don't live there anymore."

Sassy's tears renewed. "We were happy in that house. Nobody called me names or said my granddaddy is a murderer."

Sam groaned. He'd thought he'd seen every broken family situation, but this was a new one. How could he heal his daughter's pain when those who wanted to hurt her could do it simply by speaking the truth?

The blast of a high-pitched whistle cut through the air, accompanied by the floor-shaking rumble of the train pulling into the station.

"Sorry, folks, I've got work to do." Greg softened his authoritative tone with a smile. "Maybe you all can move this drama someplace else. Maybe go over to the Waffle House for breakfast."

With profuse apologies from the adults and confusion on the kids' faces, they filed out of the room. Greg stopped Sam. "You let me know how this turns out, Cuz."

Sam nodded toward Mrs. Hurst. "I have a feeling it will be all over town by noon today."

He wasn't being fair. Many caring people had turned out for the search. Of course they would be glad the kids were found. But while everybody would have questions, maybe even deserved answers, it could further hurt Sassy and Juliet. He longed to protect them from gossip, but it was probably too late.

Outside, he called to Raeder, who was buckling Peanut into his car seat. "Want to meet up at the Waffle House?" His stomach growled its agreement with the idea. "I'm buying."

"No thanks. Chores can't wait, so I need to get back to

the ranch." The cowhand waved before climbing into his truck. "See you later."

"I want to go to the Waffle House." Sassy acted as if she hadn't caused a minor riot in Riverton.

"No, ma'am, young lady." Juliet helped her into the truck's back seat. "No special treats for you today. You're going home to apologize to the sheriff and Gramma Petra." She stepped up into the back seat. "Jeff, you sit up front."

Jeff didn't hesitate. "Sure."

This was interesting. And disappointing. Either Juliet wanted to keep scolding Sassy or she just didn't want to sit next to him. Considering her attitude this entire morning, he feared it was the latter.

While Juliet called Miss Petra with the good news, Sam headed his truck back to her ranch. As they drove down the unpaved lane to the house, they met Dad's and Mom's vehicles.

Dad pulled up beside Sam's truck and lowered his window. "Petra told us you found the kids. Is it okay if we come back and—"

"Can we do that later?" Juliet called from the back seat.

Sam shrugged. "Sorry, Dad." He drove on, giving Mom a wave as he passed her. She didn't look happy, but Dad would have to tell her Juliet didn't want a family reunion at the moment.

The last of the searchers' trucks, including the sheriff's, drove past, occupants waving and sending big smiles. At the house, Sam parked in his usual spot outside the back door, and Juliet emerged with Sassy. Miss Petra ran out to greet them and grabbed Sassy into her arms, first crying, then scolding her.

Jeff didn't move to join them.

"Want to talk?"

To his shock, Jeff began to tremble. He covered his face with his hands and wept like a small child, deep, gut-wrenching sobs that almost had Sam in tears as well. Somehow he managed to let the boy exhaust his emotions without surrendering to his own.

Jeff grabbed a tissue from the dispenser on the console and blew his nose. "I messed up real bad. I wasn't trying to hurt Sassy. I love that kid." He took in a deep breath and let it out. "I wanted her to know what I learned when I was younger than her. Life stinks and you have to fight back. I wanted her to know I'll have her back. But when I think of what could have happened to her and Peanut, I want to throw up." He hiccupped, so Sam offered him a bottle of water from the packet behind the seat.

After drinking half of it, Jeff let out another long sigh. "I don't want to be like my dad. I don't want to hurt people." He shook his head. "I should have stood up for Ma. I wasn't even awake when their fight started, but when I woke up and heard them yelling, I went downstairs and saw Dad knocking Ma around. I should have stepped in to stop him from hitting her. I didn't know he'd end up—" His voice broke. "I figured it was like every time before. He'd knock her down. Then after he went to bed, I'd help her up. He'd wake up the next morning, see her bruises, realize what he'd done to her, apologize, bring flowers." Another sob. "But this time she couldn't get up. She just stared at me. But she was already gone." He gave in to tears again. "I should've stepped in," he repeated, "but I was scared he'd start in on me. Then it was too late."

Sam reached over and gripped the boy's shoulder. "You're right. He probably would have turned on you. Listen, Jeff, you can't blame yourself for your mother's death. It's solely Dill's fault. He controlled you and your mom through fear and abuse." And Juliet, too, until she managed to get free of his manipulation. "It's really hard to break a pattern of abuse in a family, but you know who can help you, don't you?"

He nodded. "I've tried to pray, but it doesn't seem to do any good. Maybe it's because *I'm* no good."

Sam lifted his own silent prayer for wisdom. "Hey, what would Miss Petra say? We're all 'no good.' We're all sinners in need of Jesus to save us."

"Yeah." Jeff grabbed another tissue and blotted his face. "I guess so. Look, I need to check on Raven. Thanks for listening."

Before Sam could think of a way to continue this conversation, Jeff jumped out of the truck. "See you later." He jogged away toward the barn.

Sam looked at his smartwatch. Ten o'clock. A lot of time left in the day. The office was closed for the fair, but he wasn't interested in rejoining the festivities. Going by himself could never measure up to the good times he'd had with Juliet and the kids yesterday. This estrangement hurt almost as much as when Juliet didn't show up ten years ago. Maybe it was time to talk to the Lord, as he'd encouraged Jeff to do. His prayer life had been a little sparse lately. Time to get back on track. "Now what, Lord?"

He glanced at the back door of the house. From the way Juliet had acted since last night, she sure didn't want him hanging around, so he started the truck and drove away. On Saturday, he'd keep his promise to Jeff about visiting Dill again, but for now, he needed to maintain his distance from her whole family. As grateful as he was over Sassy and Peanut's safe return, an ache started in his belly and rose up into his chest. And it had nothing to do with his missing breakfast.

* * *

"Honey, you gotta eat something before you go to work." Mama shoved a plate of scrambled eggs, bacon and toast in front of Juliet, then sat down across from her at the kitchen table.

Juliet picked up her fork and tried to take a bite, but her stomach rebelled. Or maybe it was her heart. She had given Sam every reason to drive away, so he had. Wasn't that what she wanted? To be shed of all the Mattsons for good? But if that was true, why had she been disappointed when the roar of his truck's motor grew quieter as he drove up the lane toward the highway?

She managed a few bites before giving up. "I need to leave." Despite poor patronage during the fair, Billings' Burgers stayed open. Juliet had suggested Jorge should buy a food truck and rent a spot on the fairgrounds, but he dismissed the idea. "Are you sure you can manage Sassy?"

Mama gave a little shrug. "Before this morning, I would have said yes. Now I'm not so sure."

"I understand. But I think she's over her hurt feelings. Or at least she realizes running away doesn't solve anything." And yet she herself had been planning to run away with the kids. What would that solve? Nothing. She needed to reassess this whole situation.

She'd moved back home shortly before Christmas partly because she'd lost her job at the Santa Fe vet clinic, but mostly because she'd needed Mama to help her straighten out her life. Of course Mama told her the only solution to her problems was to trust Jesus as her Savior, which she'd done. What an amazing difference it had made to have God in her life. He did indeed turn her life around. Then at Christmas, Dill killed Brenda, and Jeff was put in a foster home. Of course he wouldn't get along with strangers, and since she'd already been working to improve her relationship with her brother, she was there when he needed her. Which meant, to keep the judge from putting him in another foster home, she'd had to ask Sam for help. She couldn't say that was a mistake. These past few months, Jeff had made some serious progress in maturing. Plus the times they'd had together with the kids would always be precious memories for her. But what now?

Maybe her biggest beef was everybody knowing her business. As a Sizemore, she'd learned to expect the worst opinions from the people of Riverton, yet she'd tried hard to prove she was different. Now that the word was out about Sam being Sassy's father, she'd lost control of her life's narrative. And that stunk. At least she had control when it came to work. Unlike previous jobs, in this one, she could be hardworking and dependable despite her last name *and* her boss's haphazard restaurant methods. She'd done well by him, she was certain.

"Thanks for fixing this, Mama." She shoved her plate away. "But I'd better get on the road."

Before she could stand, her phone chirped with its cricket ringtone. The caller ID read "Billings' Burgers." She punched the call icon.

"Hey, Jorge. I'm on my way into town. Be there in fifteen minutes."

He coughed in that awkward way of his when he was about to give somebody bad news. "Listen, Juliet, I got this other niece here who needs a job. She's going to college and all, first one in our family, so's I promised her she could come work for me. Sorry, kid, but I'll pay you to the end of the week."

"Yeah. No problem. You take care, Jorge." She disconnected the call and burst out laughing. "Lord, You sure do have a sense of humor." Just when she'd thought she had a little bit of control over something in her life, all of a sudden, she didn't. "Okay, Lord, I surrender. What do You plan for me next?" With the way things usually went for her, no telling what it could be.

Chapter Fifteen

"**Y**ou know what you're going to say?" Sam parked his truck outside the Penitentiary of New Mexico and shut off the motor.

"Yessir." Jeff looked more confident than Sam had ever seen him. No rebellion. No attitude. It was a welcome change.

The only thing that concerned Sam was Dill's method of cutting his kids down in unexpected ways. He prayed Jeff would be able to withstand whatever manipulation his father attempted.

Inside the visitors' hall, numerous families huddled around tables with their incarcerated loved ones, attempting to gain some sort of privacy. A guard showed Jeff and Sam to a corner table. As he had before, Dill Sizemore strutted into the room like a king on his way to a coronation. Or maybe the kingpin among the prison population. Sam glanced around to see if the other prisoners gave him special notice or signaled some sort of deference to him, but they were all busy with their own visitors.

"I see you brought your nanny." Dill plunked down in the metal chair opposite Jeff and Sam, his manacled wrists clunking on the wooden table.

"No, sir." Jeff sat up straight, not wilting, and spoke in a firm tone. "I brought my lawyer, who's also my friend."

Dill blinked. "Huh. Got you fooled, eh?" He eyed Sam up and down. "But what can you expect from a Mattson? They've had it in for our family for over—"

"Yeah, yeah, I know." Jeff snorted out a laugh that sounded all too similar to his father's. "For over a hundred and forty years. Thing is, that's in the past, and we don't have to live there anymore."

Dill's eyes narrowed. "You think he's got your best interests at heart? Ain't I told you time and again, we Sizemores gotta stick together? Ain't nobody gonna take care of us but us."

"Right." Jeff inhaled a long breath. "Just like you took care of Ma."

Dill blinked again. "Now, son, we talked about this. You need to 'fess up to what you did."

"You mean calling 9-1-1 after you killed her?"

"No, now, that's not how it went down. I…"

"You what?" Exhibiting greater restraint than Sam thought possible, Jeff leaned toward Dill and glared into his eyes. "You hit her one too many times, didn't you? You thought she'd get over her head hitting the corner of the table, didn't you? Thought you could—"

Jeff inhaled another deep breath, while Sam prayed he wouldn't break down. Showing Dill any weakness wouldn't be good.

"Thought you could bring her flowers the next day, and she'd be fool enough to take you back, like always."

A hint of guilt flashed in Dill's eyes, and he slumped back in his chair. "Yeah, and she would've, too, if only—"

"Dad, when you kill somebody, life doesn't give you an 'if only.' It only gives you consequences." Jeff snorted.

"And here you are." He waved a hand to take in the room. "You always wanted to lord it over the Mattsons, but they're the ones who are helping your family recover from the mess you made."

"Now, son." Dill gave him a weak smile. "Don't you be listening to this man. He's the enemy."

"No, he's not." Jeff shook his head, his gaze at Dill not wavering. "You know, Dad, there's a way out of this for you."

Another blink. "Yeah? What?"

"You gotta turn to God. I heard they have Bible studies in this place. You need to go to one and learn about God." Jeff gave Sam a quick grin. "That's what I'm doing. You'd be surprised at how it can change your life."

Even with this welcome revelation from Jeff, Sam never expected Dill to weaken. Then his eyes misted and his posture slumped. "Maybe so." He sat up and shook himself and seemed to force his old sneer. "Well, I got things to do. You can leave now. And don't bother to come back." He lifted his hands to beckon the guard. "See you in court, kid."

As he walked away, Jeff whispered, "Yeah. See you in court." But his voice didn't waver even a little bit.

Juliet managed to duck around the corner before Sam or Jeff left the visitors' hall so they wouldn't know she'd been watching through the door's glass window. She'd followed them to the prison to protect Jeff if he needed it. But she could tell just from watching their body language during their interaction that he'd stood up for himself and had given Dill a set-down. She'd never been so proud of her brother. With both her and Jeff finally breaking free from Dill's manipulations, they could also break free from their family's long-held bad reputation. And they didn't need to run away. They could stay right here in Riverton and make the Sizemore name stand for honesty and solid citizenship right beside the Mattson name.

As much as she wanted to give Jeff a big hug and, to be fair, thank Sam for bringing her brother here, she waited until they drove away before heading home herself. She could give Jeff the affirmation he deserved after he told her about his meeting with Dill. If he told her. Maybe she could wheedle it out of him. No, that was the old Juliet. She had to let it come from him without any manipulation.

Ugh! Keeping quiet wouldn't be easy. Nor would thanking Sam for all he'd done. Maybe at church tomorrow morning she could say something to him. But what? After giving him the cold shoulder for his angry reaction to learning about Sassy, then refusing to talk to him after they found her daughter, would he even want to talk to her? She'd have to be very careful what she said to him and when she said it to avoid hurting Sassy again.

Once again, however, she lost control of the situation. On Sunday morning, they'd barely piled out of Raeder's Bronco before Linda and Andy accosted them on the church's front lawn.

"Juliet." Linda pulled her into a tight embrace. "We've got a situation here that needs clearing up before we go inside to worship the Lord. Don't you think He'd like to see us all reconciled?"

"That's what I've been telling her." Mama looped her arm around Linda's.

"We sure would like to officially welcome Sassy into our family," Andy said, "so we can start spoiling her."

At that, Sassy grinned. "I want to be spoiled."

"Yeah, I'm sure you would." Jeff tweaked Sassy's nose. "Like you're not already spoiled rotten."

"Am not!"

"Tell you what," Linda said. "After church, why don't you all come out to the ranch for dinner so we can talk through all of this?"

"Well, I—"

"Yes, we'd love to come." Mama gave Juliet a stern look. "Wouldn't we?"

"Great!" Andy patted his large black Bible, which had a dozen or so sticky notes poking out the side. "Gotta get to my Sunday school class. See y'all in the sanctuary for worship."

Raeder had already left with Peanut. Mama and Linda walked arm in arm toward the adult Sunday school building. Jeff raced off to join the three older Mattson kids, while Sassy tugged on Juliet's hand. "Can I go now? Clementine's waiting for me over there." She pointed to the youngest Mattson, who waved at Sassy.

"Oh. Okay."

With everybody else heading inside, Juliet stood in front of the church alone. She hadn't tried to find a class of her own because she just wasn't ready to go by herself. Now she had no idea where to start. Would her old reputation go before her, leading to more unwelcome comments from people like Erin Farber?

The wooden bench in the vine-covered wicker arbor by the education building seemed to beckon to her, so she walked over there to wait until worship time. She opened her Bible and read from Psalms, her new favorite book.

A half hour or more had passed when Sam leaned into the arbor. "Mind if I join you?"

Juliet jolted. That was the first thing he'd said to her

back in eighth grade. The first time he'd given her that heart-stopping smile. All these years later, he still had the power to shake her world.

"Your choice." She attempted a flippant tone, but failed. "Come on in."

"Thanks." He ducked under the leafy foliage and sat beside her. But not too close.

"Aren't you missing your class?" She tilted her head toward the building.

"Well, that's just the thing. I don't want to go alone." He gave her another devastating smile. "Want to go with me?"

In spite of the warm, fuzzy feelings trying to blossom in her heart, she shook her head. "I still have some issues to sort out before I—"

"Spend any more time with me?" He scooched closer and gently bumped his arm against hers.

She laughed. "Yes. And no." How could she get control of this conversation? But why did she want control? Easy answer. So she wouldn't get hurt again.

"I like the no part. How can we get past the yes?"

"Oh, I don't know." She stared off for a moment, then directly into his blue-green eyes. "Sam, how did we get into this situation?"

"Well, we—"

"I'll tell you."

He chuckled. "Be my guest."

"Okay, I will." She gave him a teasing smile, then grew serious. This was too important to gloss over lightly. "When we were kids, we were both rebelling against the expectations of our families. Secretly dating each other was the only way we could have any kind of control over our lives. You rebelled against the expectation that you needed to be perfect, like your dad and all the other Mattson men. So you tried being 'bad.' I rebelled against the expectation that I should join my father's crooked way of life, so I tried being 'good.'"

"I agree," Sam said. "We were trying to gain control and find our way in life for ourselves."

"Right." She nodded. As he had all those years ago, he completed her thoughts. "I know I said this before, but I'm sorry I didn't tell you about Sassy when I came back to Riverton. I was so scared of how all the Mattsons might react, especially your folks. Now I can see they're kind, loving people who want only the best for their kids, which will now include Sassy."

"You can count on it."

"But what about us, Sam?" Might as well clean the slate of all their problems.

"What about us?" It was his turn to give her a playful smile. "I kinda like having you around, even when you sneak into prison to check on your brother."

"What? You knew I was there?" She smacked his arm lightly. "Did Jeff?"

"If he did, he didn't say. You'd never make a good spy. I saw you peek around the corner in the visitors' hall, and I saw your mother's truck in the parking lot. That thing is a dead giveaway wherever you go."

"True." She laughed. "Now, about this liking to have me around. Truth is, I like having you around, too."

He slapped his knee. "That settles it, then. When do you want to get married?"

"Married?" She sat back and stared at him. "Since when did we talk about getting married?"

"Since now. Well, other than when we planned to elope." He grasped her hand and brought it up to his lips for a gentle kiss. "How about it? Let's get married and start making up for all those lost years."

"A lot happened in those lost years, Sam. I'm not sure we can—"

"Of course we can."

Heart and mind reeling, she pulled her hand back and stood. "Church will be starting soon. I'm going to find Sassy."

"Wait. What did I say?" The puzzlement on his face would have been funny if his words hadn't hurt her so much.

Did he even love her? Or did he only want to marry her to make a family for Sassy? And how could he assume she loved him enough to marry him? Even if she did, was she ready to be swallowed up into the vast Mattson clan, along with Sassy? Or was she still afraid to surrender all control of her life? She knew she could trust the Lord. People, especially the Mattsons, were another matter entirely.

The instant Juliet walked away, Sam knew what he'd done wrong. How could he make it right? He'd chase after her, only the churchyard was filling with people making their way from the Sunday school buildings to the sanctuary for worship, and he didn't want to embarrass them both by making a scene.

What a dolt he was for proposing in such a cavalier way. And he hadn't even told her he loved her. She was no longer the kid who understood his lighthearted banter, at least not about their relationship. He'd jumped ahead without taking the first and all-important step of telling her he'd fallen for her again, only this time, not as a green, needy teenager but as a grown man who knew his own mind and heart. Further, she was a grown woman who deserved all the bells and whistles—and definitely roses—that came with romance.

What now, Lord?

He wasn't surprised when Pastor Tim preached on I Corinthians 13, the very passage to answer his prayer. Like Mom and Dad would do soon, the pastor and his wife were celebrating their thirtieth wedding anniversary, and his sermon was in honor of that impressive milestone. He related stories about their marriage, some humorous, some practical, some heartbreaking, but most of all, how the Lord had brought them through it all.

As Sam listened attentively, he could see he needed to prove to Juliet that he loved her with an unselfish biblical love, love that was patient and kind and didn't insist on its own way. He especially leaned into the idea that love must bear all things and believe all things. And forgive all things, such as forgiving Juliet for not telling him about Sassy sooner. Ever since she came to his office to ask for help with Jeff, he'd been protecting his heart by not trusting that she'd changed. But she had. She'd become a believer in Jesus Christ, and now Sam must believe the best about her, not jump to conclusions as he had in thinking she'd stood him up and cheated on him. As the scripture said, he prayed he could offer her an abiding love, a love that, by the grace of God, would never end. If only she would accept him…

Juliet ate up every word of the pastor's sermon. New to reading the Bible, she hadn't read this chapter before. What an inspiration! While the passage spoke to all Christians, the pastor made it more interesting by using his own personal experience to illustrate the kind of love it referred to. So this was what marriage was all about. She tried not to glance down the pew to where Sam sat with his parents, but failed. His focus was on the pastor, and he seemed to be eating up the words as much as she was. Even in profile, he was the handsomest man she'd ever seen. But it wasn't his looks that made her love him. From the moment she approached him for help with Jeff, he'd been exhibiting the kind of love the pastor was talking about. He'd shown love, not talked about it, from his pro bono generosity as her and Jeff's lawyer to his involvement with both Jeff and Sassy in their 4-H projects. And after the way she'd hurt him, that was remarkable. What had she given in return? She'd kept the truth from him, and she'd let her pride stand in the way of reconciliation. It was time to quit such nonsense and show him a little of that biblical love. As much as she hadn't wanted to go to the ranch for dinner, now she looked forward to it. Somehow she would find a way to talk with him alone.

Before the final hymn, Pastor Tim gave his usual invitation to anyone who wanted to accept Jesus as their Savior. The organist played "I Have Decided to Follow Jesus," and the congregation joined in the song. To Juliet's surprise, Jeff came down from the balcony, walked to the front of the church and huddled with the pastor as if in prayer. Her own salvation being so recent, she wept with joy to see this final breakthrough for her brother. She wanted to join Jeff to show him her support, but knowing her brother, she decided to wait. Sam looked her way. If she wasn't mistaken, those were tears in his eyes. His smile seemed to say "Mission accomplished." She couldn't agree more. She'd prayed Jeff would have a relationship with the Lord, and now he did. And now it was time for her to repair her relationship with Sam.

* * *

After church let out, Sam took a chance and asked Juliet to let him drive Sassy out to his parents' house. After a worrisome moment of hesitation, she granted him permission. Maybe she understood that he needed to bond with their daughter in a new, meaningful way, even though he still must make amends to Juliet, too.

Sassy was agreeable to the plan, almost excited to ride in his truck. But as they drove out of town, she was strangely quiet in the front seat beside him, and he wasn't sure how to begin. *Lord, show me the way.*

"Mr. Sam, are you embarrassed about being my daddy? I mean, me being a Sizemore and all?"

Sam's eyes misted over, and he had difficulty focusing on the road ahead. "Not at all, Sassy. I'm so proud of you and proud to be your dad." He wanted to tell her she was a Mattson, too, but that was a conversation for later.

She was quiet again for several minutes. "Why are you proud of me?"

The plaintive tone in her voice alerted him that this was an important issue to her. A glib, tossed-off answer wouldn't give her any sense of security. Again, he prayed for wisdom.

"Sweetheart, remember when you trusted Jesus as your Savior?"

A half smile appeared. "Uh-huh."

"Well, Jesus loves you more than you can measure. In fact, God made you a unique person, and He has a plan for your life. Part of that plan is the family you were born into…who your parents are, your mom and me. God puts a special love in parents so they can raise their kids knowing Him. There's a Bible verse that says we are able to love others because He first loved us."

"But my granddaddy doesn't love…" She grew quiet again.

Talking about Dill wouldn't help her feel secure, so Sam tried to bring her back to what would.

"Oh, Sassy, your granddaddy's got something broken inside him. We can pray he'll find out about God's love. But you know your mom loves you, and now you know I love you just because you're you." He chuckled for effect. "As for my being proud of you, well, not only are you smart and funny, but you're very responsible for a nine-year-old. Look at the way you take care of your baby chicks."

"And Peanut. I take care of Peanut."

Now Sam laughed for real. "Yeah, well, just don't take him on any more adventures like you did yesterday."

Her impish grin appeared. "I think I learned my lesson. So, can I call you Daddy?"

Sam's eyes misted again. "Yes. Please do." He drove into his usual parking place at home and hurried around to help her out of the truck.

She jumped into his arms. "I love you, Daddy." Her fierce hug around his neck sent a flood of joy through his heart.

"I love you, too, Sassy."

As she had before, Linda had prepared dinner ahead of time, this time with lasagna and salad on the menu, along with the ever-present sweet tea. Seated around the long table, the Sizemores and Mattsons, as Andy would say, broke bread together. Juliet shifted in her chair. She'd much rather take Sam aside and apologize right away and ask for his forgiveness. From the way he avoided her gaze since they arrived at the ranch, she would have some work to do on that score. Or maybe he was just too involved with

Sassy to look her way. In fact, Juliet was pleased to see their interaction. Good thing she'd let Sassy ride out here to the ranch with him.

After giving thanks for the food, in his usual fashion, Andy asked the kids what they learned from the sermon.

Sassy raised her hand. "We're supposed to love everybody. I love Clementine. She's my friend. But I'm gonna have to try real hard to love Ginny Gray when she's mean to me."

Andy winked at her. "You just ask the Lord for help, sweetheart, and He'll show you what to do." He turned to Jeff. "How about you? Looked like you made a decision today."

"Yessir. Like the song says, I've decided to follow Jesus." He shrugged. "And like Sassy says, it's easier to love a friend who's good to you, so I'm gonna have a hard time loving my dad after he—" He glanced at Sassy. "Well, you know."

"I'm sure that'll take some work, son," Andy said. "But the Lord will show you the way." He gave Juliet a paternal smile. "Would you mind if Sassy calls us Grampa and Gramma? That is, if she wants to?"

"I want to." Sassy jumped down from her chair and hurried to the head of the table, plunging herself into his open arms. "I love you, Grampa."

His eyes suspiciously red, Andy gave her a gentle squeeze. "I love you, too, sweetheart."

Sassy ran to the other end of the table and wrapped her arms around Linda's neck. "I already have a Gramma, so can I call you Grammy?"

Linda, also shedding tears, nodded. "Of course you can, honey. And you know what? You are our very first grandchild."

Mama looked on with a satisfied smile. "Praise the Lord."

"Praise the Lord and pass the dessert," Andy said. "If the rumors are true, it's homemade blueberry ice cream."

After the meal, Mama and Linda shooed Juliet out of the kitchen.

"We'll clean up," Mama said. "You go mend fences with that man of yours."

"Well, not exactly my man, Mama." Juliet looked out the dining room window and saw Sam and his dad sitting in wicker chairs under a cottonwood tree.

They'd already sent the kids over to the Big House to spend time with Sassy's cousins and Jeff's new best friends. Seemed like there was only one fence to mend. She went outside to join the men.

"Hey, guys. What's happening?"

Both men stood.

Andy glanced at her, then Sam. "I'm gonna get down to the barn and make sure...well, whatever." He strode off chuckling to himself.

"What was that all about?" Juliet looked up into Sam's blue-green eyes, which were accentuated by his turquoise dress shirt. "Never mind. I came out here to tell you..."

"I love you."

"I love you."

They spoke at the same time, then laughed together.

"I'm sorry—"

"I'm sorry—"

Again, they spoke at the same time.

"Oh, Sam, I will mar—"

"Shh." He put a finger on her lips, knelt in front of her and took her hand. "Miss Juliet Anne Sizemore, will you marry me?"

Some day she would tell him her middle name was actually Angelique, but she wouldn't ruin this moment by correcting him. "Well, of course I will. Like you said, it's time we started making up for all those lost years."

He stood and pulled her into his arms, then brushed a hand across her cheek. Until that moment, she hadn't realized she was crying.

"I love you so much, Jules. I love Sassy, and I'm so proud of the way you've raised her. We're going to make a great family." He grew thoughtful. "This time I want to do everything properly, but I sure don't want to ask your father's blessing. How about I ask Sassy?"

"And Jeff?"

"And Jeff, of course. If not for him, we wouldn't be here today." Sam tucked a wayward strand of her hair behind her ear, his touch causing her skin to tingle. "So…" He gave her a teasing grin. "Do I have to wait for their approval before I kiss you?"

"Probably should. But I don't have to wait to kiss you." She rose up on her tiptoes and planted a quick one on his lips. They tasted of blueberry ice cream.

"Oh, that was nice." He pulled her closer for another kiss that lasted quite a bit longer.

"Hey!" Sassy's unmistakable voice broke into Juliet's thoughts. "You're kissing my mom. Did I say you could kiss my mom?"

"Hey, cut it out, Sass." Jeff stood behind her. "Don't you want them to get married?"

Sassy crossed her arms. "I don't know. Daddy, will you promise not to yell at my mom again?"

Sam cleared his throat. "Well, I'd like to promise that, but you never know—"

"Married people don't always agree." Juliet broke away

from Sam and gathered her daughter into her arms. "Sometimes they argue. It's okay." She glanced at Jeff, whose troubled expression made her heart ache. "Not every argument ends badly, guys. People need to work things out God's way, but it doesn't mean they don't get upset and raise their voices."

"Sweetheart." Sam took Sassy's hand. "I can promise you I'll try very hard never to cause your mom or you any pain." He looked at Jeff. "Or you."

Jeff managed a smile. "I believe you." He nudged Sassy's arm. "Go on. Say it."

Sassy rolled her eyes. "Okaaay." She hugged Sam's waist.

Sam lifted her into a big hug and swung her around. "Sassy, I love you so much."

She giggled. "I love you, too. When are you and Mommy getting married?"

Sam set her down and took Juliet's hand. "When do you want to?"

Juliet's heart felt near to bursting. "Can't we just keep to the original plan and elope?"

Sam folded her into his arms again. "Aw, sweetheart, let's do it up big this time. I want everybody in this town to know that Samuel Grant Mattson loves Juliet Anne Sizemore and is proud of it. Let's have the biggest wedding Riverton's ever seen?"

She buried her face in his chest and murmured, "Sounds like a plan."

The early-June sun shone down on Sam and his soon-to-be family as they climbed the courthouse steps. The school year had ended two days ago, and Jeff had insisted they must take care of business with the judge before the wedding. This time, Sam felt no doubt or hesitation over committing to be responsible for Jeff. He'd always wanted a brother, and now he would have one.

Sassy and Miss Petra had asked to witness the event. Juliet had agreed, but only after they both promised not to be their usual chatty selves in front of the judge.

As before, a professionally dressed assistant ushered them into Judge Mathis's chambers. The woman looked up from paperwork and gave them a half-smile, a rare gesture on her part.

"Welcome, folks. Have a seat." She waved a hand toward the chairs in front of her desk, then got right down to business. "Jeff, I'm proud of you. You've come a long way in a short time, and your sister and Sam tell me your improvements are genuine." She glanced at them, then refocused on Jeff. "Do you want me to grant them permanent guardianship to be in effect until you turn eighteen?"

Jeff sat up straight. "Yes, ma'am. And Mama Petra, too."

Sam heard soft gasps coming from Juliet and her mother. He was just as surprised to hear Jeff acknowledge Miss Petra's influence in his life, not to mention calling her Mama.

"Well, that's interesting." The judge peered down at her papers again. "You okay with that, Petra?"

Miss Petra cleared her throat. "Oh, yes, Gladys... I mean, yes, ma'am, Judge Mathis."

The judge's eyes twinkled, and she hid a smile. "Very well. I'll make a note of it. With all of you looking out for Jeff, I'm sure he's on the right path."

Not for the first time, Sam was amazed at Miss Petra's goodness to this boy whose birth had broken up her marriage fifteen years ago.

Despite her promise to be quiet, Sassy stood and walked

to the desk. "I want to be on the right path, too, Miss Judge. Can you make Sam my legal daddy?"

Sam traded a look with Juliet. They'd already talked about this but hadn't told Sassy. Even now the paperwork, including her birth certificate naming him as her father, sat in a file on his desk at the law office. The task would be completed before the wedding.

The judge blinked, then gave Sassy a gentle smile. "From what I hear, you're already on the right path, sweetheart." She glanced at Sam, then Juliet. "But we're going to make it official that Sam's your daddy. Okay?"

"Okay." Sassy grinned, then turned to Sam. "Can we go for ice cream, Daddy?"

Now the judge, and everyone else, laughed out loud.

"Looks like you're gonna have your hands full, Mr. Mattson. I wish you—" she looked at Juliet "—all of you— the very best."

His heart still soaring with joy at hearing Sassy call him Daddy, Sam could barely manage to answer. "Thank you, Judge."

Epilogue

One week later on a bright Saturday morning, Sam stood at the front of the church sanctuary beside his Cousin Will. After a bit, he shifted his stance from one foot to the other. What was taking Juliet so long? The organist had already begun to play the wedding march when an usher whispered something to her. She then returned to Pachelbel's "Canon in D Major," which she'd played while guests filed into the pews.

What had happened? Had Juliet changed her mind? Would she fail to meet him again? Sam cast a nervous glance around the packed sanctuary. At least the first time she hadn't shown up to marry him, only their parents had known about it. If she did it again, the whole town would know. Never mind what they thought. He doubted he could ever get over another broken heart.

He glanced at Will, who shrugged and gave him a sympathetic smile. "Want me to go find out what the problem is?"

"Uh, well…" He turned to Pastor Tim, whose face conveyed his usual calm and patience.

"I'm sure it will be all right," he whispered.

Sure enough, it was. The double doors to the center aisle opened, and little Peanut walked in carrying a white pillow with two wedding rings attached with silk ribbons. Head held high, he walked with purpose toward the front. Halfway there, he stopped and turned around.

"Come on, Sassy!"

Muted chuckles swept through the room as Sassy came through the door tossing white rose petals from her basket into the air. "You're supposed to keep walking," she said in a not-too-quiet voice.

As if he just realized he was the center of everyone's attention, his eyes widened. "You come with me."

Sassy huffed impatiently. "Okay. Let's go."

Side by side, the two children made their way clear to the front, with Peanut using one hand to clutch the pillow and the other to help Sassy toss the flowers.

Sam's knees almost gave way as relief flooded his chest.

Will caught his elbow and chuckled softly. "Hang in there, Cuz."

Next to enter the sanctuary was Juliet's matron of honor, Jenna Williams, Miss Petra's cousin from Colorado, who had helped raise Sassy those first years. At last, the wedding march began again, and Juliet entered on Jeff's arm. While the teen looked handsome in his brand-new tan Western suit and new brown boots, it was Juliet who held Sam's attention.

A wave of dizziness swept through him, and his knees again threatened to buckle...until Will nudged him and whispered, "Take a breath."

Inhaling quickly, he could finally focus on his bride. She hadn't stood him up after all.

Wow! What a perfect portrait of class, nostalgia and modesty. Her white, Western-style mid-length dress had one of those pretty, raggedy hemlines and long lace sleeves, and fit her slim, curvy figure perfectly. She wore white cowgirl boots with sparkling rhinestones that caught the morning light filtering in through the side windows. And her white Western hat would draw anyone's attention, with its lacy veil streaming from its side and back.

But it was her gorgeous face on which Sam settled his gaze. He'd never seen a more beautiful sight. When she reached him and gave him her glorious smile, it was all he could do not to kiss her right then and there.

He was pretty sure they made it through the ceremony, because he heard Pastor Tim say, "I now pronounce you husband and wife. Sam, you may kiss your bride."

And so he did. The kiss must have lasted a bit long, because Pastor Tim chuckled and tapped Sam on the shoulder, then turned the two of them to face the congregation.

"Ladies and gentlemen, I present to you Mr. and Mrs. Sam Mattson."

Applause broke out in the congregation, which included members of both Mattson and Sizemore families. The Mattson clan had invited everyone to a barbecue on the church lawn. And Sam felt pretty sure nobody would turn them down, no matter what their last name was.

Before they cut their three-tiered cake, Sam needed one question answered. "What was the delay? You had me worried."

"Aww. I'm sorry." Juliet reached up to kiss his cheek. "It was something blue."

"Huh?" He scratched his head. "That's a new one."

She laughed. "I had my something old. Mama's silver pin from her mama." She touched the pink tourmaline and filigree pin at her neckline. "Something new is my dress. Well, my whole outfit. Something borrowed, Cousin Jenna's lace hanky." She pulled it from her sleeve. "But I forgot to find something blue." She quirked a cute little smile. "Our daughter was very impatient with me. Finally she said, 'Mommy, your blue eyes will have to do. Let's go get married!'"

Sam chuckled, then laughed out loud. "I have a feeling that kid is going to keep us on our toes."

"Yep." Juliet nodded. "I wouldn't have it any other way."

And neither would Sam.

Was this the end of the hundred-and-forty-year Mattson–Sizemore feud? Sam and Juliet had already been praying that it would be. But only time would tell.

* * * * *

*Enjoy these previous contemporary romances
by Louise M. Gouge
about the Mattson family:*

Safe Haven Ranch
A Faithful Guardian

Available now from Love Inspired!

Dear Reader,

Thank you for choosing *Feuding with the Cowboy*. I hope you enjoyed reading the love story of Sam Mattson and Juliet Sizemore, who live along the Rio Grande in my fictional town of Riverton, New Mexico.

This book is a legacy sequel to my Love Inspired Historical novella, *Yuletide Reunion*, published in the anthology *A Western Christmas* (2015), two LIH novels, *Finding Her Frontier Family* (2022) and *Finding Her Frontier Home* (2023), and my contemporary Love Inspired books, *Safe Haven Ranch* (2024) and *A Faithful Guardian* (2024). I started with a family of five Mattson brothers back in the 1880s. Each one found his lady love and lived happily ever after.

So it's time to see what's happened to some of the many descendants of these fine Christian characters. Back in those Wild West days, there were some bad guys in Riverton, too, namely, the Sizemores, who liked to cause trouble for the Mattsons. It's not surprising when their many descendants follow in the family's criminal ways. Like the Hatfields and McCoys, the Mattsons and Sizemores have a generational feud going on. But maybe, just maybe, some of the younger generation can bridge the gap and, maybe, just maybe, find a way to end the feud once and for all.

I love to hear from my readers, so if you enjoyed *Feuding with the Cowboy*, please write and let me know. Please also visit my website: louisemgougeauthor.blogspot.com, find me on Facebook: facebook.com/LouiseMGouge Author or follow me on BookBub: bookbub.com/profile/ louise-m-gouge.

God bless you.
Louise M. Gouge

Get up to 4 Free Books!

We'll send you 2 free books from each series you try PLUS a free Mystery Gift.

FREE Value Over **$25**

Both the **Love Inspired®** and **Love Inspired® Suspense** series feature compelling novels filled with inspirational romance, faith, forgiveness and hope.